"A vivid portrait of the cultures and social realities of Islamic North Africa. A moving story, perhaps a tragedy, set in a fascinating and thought-provoking context."
Felicity Yates, *Gay Community News*

"An affair of stellar lust and deadly attrition . . . the novel is exhilarating and expansive. Shortland has used her intimate knowledge of the Touareg to paint the necessarily recondite and exquisitely detailed background – and for this alone the book should be read."
Mary Finn, *RTE Guide*

"A mesmerising, exquisitely-written story of love and betrayal, set against the vast and corrupt backdrop of Africa."
Marian Keyes, Author of *Watermelon, Lucy Sullivan is Getting Married, Rachel's Holiday* and *Last Chance Saloon*

PRAISE FOR *MIND THAT 'TIS MY BROTHER*

"The Irish Tourist Board should reprint thousands of copies and use them as promotional material – bugger the Blarney Stone."
Carl Miller, *Time Out*

"The madness of obsession and the undying lust of the spirit are portrayed in scenes that are bound to offend. I loved it."
Bill Hughes, Director, *Radius Television (Irish Times)*

"A Corkonian Roddy Doyle, with an equally exact ear for the way people speak, but with a more subversive sense of humour . . . "
Sinéad Mooney, *The Examiner*

"Outrageous characterisations abound in this hugely enjoyable first novel . . . a comic masterpiece."
Junior Larkin, *Gay Community News*

"She writes with the authority of a gay man, which is staggering considering she is a straight woman."
*QX* (London)

"Just one or two lines of Gaye's dialogue justify the price of the book . . . Her books are also very sexy reads."
Michael Carson, Author of *Sucking Sherbet Lemons* and *Dying in Style*

"If she continues in the same rich vein Shortland could well become to Cork what Maupin is to San Francisco."
Tony Leonard, *Thud* (London)

"New implausibles are established with increasing frequency in the ferment of Irish culture: here is . . . an Irish stew well seasoned with transvestism and alcoholism, not forgetting descriptions of gay sex that range from the bizarre by way of the hysterical to the transcendent."
*Our Times* (London)

### PRAISE FOR *TURTLES ALL THE WAY DOWN*

"Mad entirely . . . dialogue to die for . . . This isn't one to read on the bus if you value your reputation for sober citizenship; on the other hand it could restore your faith in life, the universe and whatever you're having yourself."
Helen Byrne, *RTE Guide*

"Irvine Welsh should be taking lessons from Gaye Shortland. You'll laugh, you'll cry, you're unlikely to recommend it to your granny. She's not out spotting trains, she's in the driving seat, effortlessly achieving on every page a cocktail of loud music, rough sex and gritty prose that relegates Welsh and his mob to the anorak class."
Sinéad Mooney, *The Examiner*

"One of the funniest books I had read for a long time . . . funny enough to make me catch my breath and scream aloud with laughter. Not dissimilar to Roddy Doyle . . . in a style which echoes the manic reality of the characters of Flann O'Brien. But Gaye Shortland is, in my opinion, a superior writer."
Clare Toolan, *fm*

"I loved it. The true test, I suppose, is that while I was reading it at home, lots of times I actually cracked up laughing out loud on my own, so – thumbs up."

Pat O'Mahony, *The Daily Record*, RTE Radio One

"Shortland's gift for describing the tenderness and physical concentratedness of sex (even where one partner is disembodied) . . . her ability to convey what is decent, even heroic, in her scuzziest characters."

*Gay Community News*

"It's doubtful that anyone in Ireland would have the courage to [film] it: we'll wait for Channel 4 to do it, and then buy it off them."

*The Phoenix*

"Gaye Shortland is a contemporary writer in every sense of the word."

Olaf Tyaransen, *Hot Press*

"An extraordinary outpouring . . . the book's energy and anarchy are refreshing, as is its exuberant treatment of gay sex . . . "

Arminta Wallace, *The Irish Times*

"An Irish Irvine Welsh with emphasis on queens rather than junkies . . . the cast of characters is so strong each of them could almost warrant a book of their own. Like the Welsh books, once you get the accent in your head, it flows like a gurgling river and will have you laughing out loud . . . "

*QX Magazine International*

"An addictive mix of sexiness and comedy . . . "

Sharon Barnes, *In Dublin*

"A startlingly original and wildly humorous jaunt . . . Gaye Shortland is one of Ireland's most talented writers . . . "

Marian Keyes, *IT* (*Irish Tatler*)

# NORTH AFRICA

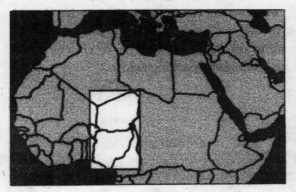

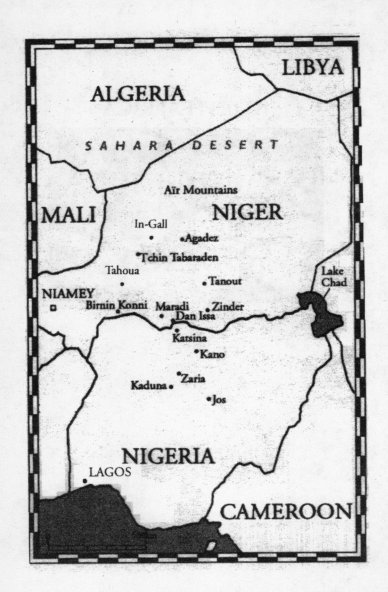

# Harmattan

# Harmattan

## GAYE SHORTLAND

POOLBEG

Published 1999 by
Poolbeg Press Ltd
123 Baldoyle Industrial Estate
Dublin 13, Ireland

© Gaye Shortland 1999

The moral right of the author has been asserted.

**The Arts Council**
An Chomhairle Ealaíon

A catalogue record for this book is available from the British Library.

ISBN 1 85371 940 4

Cover photography by Gaye Shortland
Illustrations by Sarah Farrelly
Cover design by Artmark
Set by Poolbeg Group Services Ltd in Goudy 11/14.5
Printed by The Guernsey Press Ltd,
Vale, Guernsey, Channel Islands.

www.poolbeg.com

A Note on the Author

Born in Cork, Ireland, Gaye Shortland has taught
English literature at University College Cork, the
University of Leeds, Ahmadu Bello University Nigeria
and the Université de Niamey in Niger. She lived for
fifteen years in Africa, spending much of that time with
the nomadic Tuareg of the Sahara and eventually
abandoning teaching in favour of managing a restaurant
for the American Embassy in Niamey. She married a
Tuareg and has three children. Now living in Cork, she
is the author of three critically acclaimed novels: *Mind
That 'tis My Brother* and *Turtles All the Way Down*, set in
Cork, and *Polygamy*, set in Africa.

To my sister Jackie and my daughter Maryam,
Who lived my Sahara with me.
Jac: I wish you heaven.
Miri: May you find your Sahara.

And hell, why not?
To Nicky again.

# Eclipse

❧❧❧❧❧

At midday yesterday brave men were parading
And happy were the wearers of long hair-tresses;
When afternoon prayertime came
And mallams were about to pray
A windstorm blew from the north,
A most terrible and fearsome one that soared into the sky
And fell down clogging up chests.
I saw the sun shoot out, blurred by foggy shades,
Stars were squeezed out into bold relief by darkness
And gazed at the whole world to our greatest amazement;
They stood motionless like startled gazelles.
Armed men were contemplating flight,
All the evil ones on that day looked most disturbed,
This dreadful moment is Judgment Day, they thought.
Young women, that day, fell out with noble men,
Happy were the slaves – they looked not the least distraught –
But others, in despair, were overwhelmed by thoughts of death.
Some said: The Ruler of the World has terminated it.
Could it be the moon, some wondered, that's covered it up?
And others explained: the sun has been eclipsed by its Lord.

As for me, I rode a mighty camel, swift and large-eared,
In the company of Maryama.

(from the Tamajegh)

❧❧❧❧❧

1

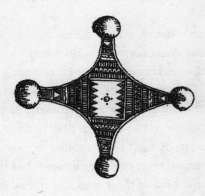

# Prologue/Epilogue

*Croagh Patrick, Mayo, West of Ireland*

I was still on the lower reaches of the mountain when I saw
the first pair of bare feet: white and raw under the rolled-
up trouser-ends, feeling out a foothold in the mud and
stones. This was what I had been waiting for. Now I could
do it without feeling a fool.

I sat down at once and took off my sodden runners and socks and stuffed them into the outside pocket of my back-pack. Carrying too much again. Like always. Next time I'd have sense — I already knew there would be a next time.

I started off again, leaning into the support of the pilgrim staff. It wasn't too bad. A lot of the path was mud, warm and comforting underfoot — my jeans were soon caked with it — but the fear of slipping in the mud set up a muscular tension and soon I was picking out footholds of rock and stone instead.

There weren't many others doing it barefoot. For the most part I was overtaken by wellington boots, runners, climbing-boots, Sunday-best and even teetering high-heels. A group of German hikers tramped past, somehow ridiculous in their expensive and efficient rain-gear, here among the headscarves and cheap plastic raincoats, the T-shirts and nylon stockings. Their tanned faces were sallow in the rain and glaringly out of their element; but the pink and freckled Irish, the blue of their eyes and the peaty colours of their hair belonged here on this mountain — they had been doing this climb for thousands of years before the god Lugh was supplanted by Patrick. Awesome.

A stream crossed the path. I waded in. It wasn't too cold. Jimmy Cliff crossing his rivers.

And as always, with the song, came the sound of the African silence — a dryness that whispered almost subliminally through the grasses and leaves and sand — and I was wending through the scrub with "Many Rivers to Cross" spiralling into the vastness, my own private soundtrack. The laughter. The Land Cruiser heaved gently over the sand and the opening credits rolled up over the screen. I hit a bad rut and the heads of the guys in the back slammed against the roof. *"Fuck you, Ellen!"* shouted young Ilyas in Tamajegh. *"I'll be feeling that until I'm fifty!"*

And, as always, his laughing face was more vivid, more real than anything around me, than the rain in my face, than the mud under my feet, than the gasping figures passing me on their upward or downward trek.

I climbed.

Was it just that the African sunlight had imprinted the images indelibly on my brain? Or had the people there a stronger presence? Here in the Irish mist, would Ilyas shine?

I had passed the statue of Patrick way back and now reached the first Station, *Leacht Benain,* where pilgrims reciting the prescribed numbers of *Our Father's* and *Hail Mary's* and *Glory-Be's* knelt and shuffled around a marker – a heap of stones. Would I miss out on the magic if I didn't fulfil the ritual? I was wearing my grandmother's wooden rosary beads around my neck . . .

I paused and looked back through the rain at the great sweep of Clew Bay.

I pushed on, itching to take out my Walkman, needing music. Well, why not? What, after all, if I had a hankering to hear the Latin Mass? A few Gregorian chants? Hadn't the age of technology come to Croagh Patrick yet?

Yes, it had. Stalking through the mist up ahead of me were the yellow-slickered, yellow-haired figures of a camera crew. Tall, Teutonic supermen, on a working vacation from Valhalla. One of them wedged himself between some rocks by the edge of the path and the huge phallic camera focused on my feet as I passed. I was by now in pain – I couldn't stop to give the camera the come-hither.

Fame.

Jesus. The Walkman. I needed Prince to get me up this mountain.

It had begun to rain heavily. I was sweating in my light thigh-length raincoat. Maybe I'd be better without it.

*"Keep back! Keep back there, please!"* The shout was urgent.

A group of uniformed First Aiders came down the path carrying a stretcher. The man in it was grey-faced, motionless, bleeding from the nose. His eyes were closed. A stroke? Or had he simply fallen and broken every bone in his body? I shook with a series of little gasping giggles – it was so bizarre and unexpected – but at the same time my skin crawled with the shock of seeing it.

I began to climb again.

A black T-shirt passed by, a curly-haired guy climbing with the vigour of young muscles, his sweater tied around his waist. *If You Have A Stiffy – Use A Jiffy*, said the T-shirt. Jesus, it must be something else to be a man. There had to be a God. And he had to be the Original Mad Scientist to think up something as bizarre as the male erection. I could see him, steaming in a purple kitsch bath like The Purple One in the video – his eyes were closed but a little smile quirked at the corners of his lips – he was indulging in his soaring passion for outrageous invention. What was Lugh's forte? I didn't know the mythology. I vaguely remembered him having a significant mother. Hadn't they all?

There was a First Aid tent to the right of the path. I sat on a convenient stone outside it and dragged my raincoat off.

"Are you all right?" asked one of the uniformed young

First Aiders. He wore a black beret and a cute teenage smile.

"Grand. Just hot."

My T-shirt said *Dangerous Tour 92*. "Dangerous" – language was so fucking wonderful – words invented and re-invented. "This is as *bad* as it gets," I muttered. I pulled out my camera and gave it to the guy with the smile, to take my picture as I sat there in the rain on the rock. *I Was Here*. My mother would want to see it.

"Get the smile and the feet," said another young black-beret, his freckled face grinning around the tent-flap.

Everyone was very gay on this mountain – there was a corrupted word – hijacked – shanghaied. A bright-eyed old woman smiled at me as she passed, her nylon-clad legs, thin as two sticks, pushing her on. A giggling girl swayed by on high-heeled sandals, hauled onwards and upwards by two laughing young men.

I snapped and managed to get the high-heeled young legs and the stick-thin ones beyond. The speed would probably be wrong, though.

"How do the old people do it?" I asked Cute Smile.

His grin became wider. "They think if they do it today they'll live to do it again next year!"

I packed my camera and raincoat away, planted my ash-staff in the mud and pushed myself to my feet. I climbed. So far I couldn't see where this mountain had earned its fearsome reputation. It wasn't so hard. Even in bare feet.

As if in answer to the thought another stretcher came down the path, a woman this time, comatose. I stepped back and the group passed, the woman again grey-faced, motionless. Were they sedated?

I climbed.

"How're yeh doin'?" A bunch of professionals – boots, ropes, rucksacks and woolly caps. The male bonding was thick enough to smell it. The speaker was long-nosed, small and wiry.

"Fine, thanks!"

"'Tis hard enough without doin' it in yer bare-ahs!" A Corkman. From my city.

"Is it so hard? Really? It's just a hill-walk, isn't it?" I said, lengthening my stride with difficulty.

He laughed, almost strolling in his climbing boots in comparison to my straining efforts. "'Tis only two thousand five hundred feet but in my opinion 'tis harder and more dangerous than Carrauntoohil. And I've climbed Carrauntoohil many a time."

"What's so dangerous about it exactly?" My breath was heaving in my effort to keep up with him. "What's happening up there? Those stretchers are putting the fear of God on me."

"You'll see when yeh come to it! The top a' the mountain is a huge cone of scree but not the usual small stones – these are big jagged pieces that slide under yer feet. Hang on to that staff – yeh're goin' to need it!" He was falling behind his group. "Right! See yeh at the top!"

"Hey!" I called, reluctant to let him go. "How many people d'yeh reckon are doing this climb today?"

"Dunno! It'll be in the papers tomorrow!" he called over his shoulder.

"But, usually like," I shouted. "On Reek Sunday?"

"About forty thousand!" the answer came back.

"Who counts them?" But he was gone.

But here surely was the statistician who did the counting. He had a trim haircut, spectacles and a buff knee-length coat. In his right hand he held a black umbrella. No pilgrim staff. In his other hand was a small wooden case, well-polished, such as one might carry papers in.

"Would you like a sandwich?" he asked.

"Eh, eh yes, I would," I answered, intrigued.

"Come over here then."

Weren't we supposed to be fasting?

It had stopped raining. The mist was thick though patchy. I was drenched to the skin. We stepped off the path on the higher side and climbed a little through the heather. He sat down on a rock and closed his umbrella smartly. I sat. Why am I doing this? The last thing I want is a sandwich. That case – what did he have in there? Surely not innocent sandwiches. His butterfly collection? A dismembered infant?

He threw back the lid. Sandwiches. He handed me a cheese sandwich. We sat there eating. The mist swirled round and then cleared for a startling breathtaking moment – an awesome drop, the vivid blue of lakes tiny at the bottom of the rocky valley.

"Did yeh see that?" asked the statistician. "That's the lake Saint Patrick banished the snakes into. He threw his bell at them and they all vanished into it. And the toads too."

"Toads? I never heard that."

"Oh, yeah, there are no toads in Ireland – or only one type, the natterjack, and not many of them. Oh, yes, Patrick did a good job while he was at it." He sighed. "On a clear day you can see the whole of Clew Bay from the top," he said. "We've no luck."

"Hey!" Shrilly. An anoraked woman with a blonde ponytail and two children in tow was climbing to the right where the path had taken a sharp turn upwards. They looked in profile as if they were crawling up on hands and knees. She had paused, hands planted on the rocks, glaring. "You're not supposed to eat on the mountain! 'Tis against the rules!"

*Fuck you, lady.* The Americans had a succinct word for it. I had seen dozens of people flashing Coca-Cola cans. "Where are they getting the coke?" I asked the statistician.

"There's a Coca-Cola stand at the top."

I loved it. "You're not serious! How do they get the stuff up there?"

"Oh, by donkey."

I chuckled. "The Great God Coke . . . "

"Lugh?" He had misheard me. "Ah . . . it's his day if we did but know it. Another sandwich?"

I shook my head. *Lughnasa,* the end of summer. When? I always confused it – July? Or August? "It's August, isn't it? *Lughnasa?*"

"Yes. Next week."

The ancient god heaved in the heart of the mountain.

"There's gold in the mountain, you know," he went on. "But the government won't let them touch it. The mountain is sacred, they say."

The Tourist Industry? Still an' all, fair dues to the government. A spirit of devilment made me test him. "How much gold is there?"

"Overall grades of zero point five ounces per ton – in at least twelve quartz veins. It could produce a minimum of 700,000 tons of ore." He nodded vigorously.

"Oh, that's impressive!" I breathed, laying it on heavily.

"Info Freako" . . . Jesus Jones . . . The figures meant nothing to me but I was smiling inwardly with the joy of it – the statistician knew his facts. My flesh began to crawl with pleasure and I knew this was one of the moments. Keep him talking. "Eh, what's the geological composition of the mountain?" Good one, that.

"Silurian Quartzite. Highly resistant. Probably the cone, the conical peak, suffered aerial erosion when it protruded over the last ice sheet. The scree slopes are typical of that . . . " He was away.

I was now listening with only a layer of my brain. I nodded and showed interest and kept him going. But I was listening to my body and the inward eye was elsewhere.

I was back in my grandmother's bed inside the sitting-room window, tingling with pleasure, cuddled against the old woman's body in the pink flannel nightdress soft and warm and smelling of talcum-powder, watching her lips tell the story as the slightly lisping sibilants went on and on.

I shivered now with pleasure, beginning to feel the tension in my genitals. But he had paused. I mustn't let him stop. "There's a chapel up there, isn't there?" I said swiftly.

"Yes, there's Mass – the priest does the climb in the dark before dawn. Everyone did it at night in the old days – in fact, right up to the seventies – but they won't allow that any more. Too dangerous." He stood up, snapping his case shut.

I'd lost him.

He picked up his umbrella. "Well, I'd better be off. Nice talking to you."

"Thanks for the sandwich. And the chat."

I followed him, cutting across the heather to the path. It was rougher now, steeper. It hurt underfoot. I had to put my back into it. I was still distracted by the hum of sensuality in my body. I began to fantasise but discovered Clint wasn't going to get me up this mountain – not even if I imagined him waiting for me at the top. Banish Eastwood with the snakes.

"Aren't you a glutton for punishment?" A cheerful red-haired nun was passing me – there were two, nodding and smiling down at my bare feet. They weren't wearing veils. I knew they were nuns only by the uniform grey and the silver crosses swinging from their necks. "You must have committed some terrible sins to need to do that!"

I grinned back. Mortification of the flesh must be out of fashion in the convents.

*No sins. I like the pain. It seems.*

They slowed to my barefoot pace. I'd better come up with some chat. "Well, y'see," I said, "my first great passion in life was Saint Philomena, Heroine and Martyr." She of the rose-red robe with coordinated accessories – a pink garland, a clutch of arrows and an anchor at her feet.

The nuns grinned in unison, the second one flashing an impressive set of buck teeth.

"And from there I got the notion life was all about being pierced with arrows. I was right about that." I'd never got over the taste for boyish hips and chests either.

The nuns guffawed.

"And to think she was struck off the list!" said the red-haired one.

"Ah, yes – " Vatican Two had done its spring-cleaning and poor Philomena had been swept out with the new broom.

"After all the devotion people had to her! To decide she didn't exist at all!" said the buck-toothed one. "It's a shame really."

The conversation was punctuated by little gasps and pants as we climbed.

"Yes, it is. After all, a myth is as good as the real thing . . ." That was a bit close to the bone, I thought, glancing at the nuns out of the corner of my eye. "I still have her statue."

"Those were the good old days," said the first nun.

"Good old days?" I wouldn't let anyone get away with that. "Wearing headscarves to show submission? Quaking with terror before that dark Confessional box . . ." Having to grit the teeth and go through your fear. Nowadays an adult would be put on Valium for less stress. The bit of extra emotion had made my breath come short.

"And the days of the long fast from midnight before Holy Communion," said the buck-toothed nun.

"Oh, that was ridiculous!" gasped the other. "And for children – who were fasting from maybe eight o'clock the night before!"

"Yes." It was really hard to place my feet on the stones and keep up this breezy chat. "God, that used to kill me. I can still remember the dry stickiness of the host in my mouth and the church starting to heave around me and knowing I was going to faint again." I had hated and feared it. Yet as a budding masochist it felt appropriate when I fainted clean out every Sunday to the buzz of extraterrestrial voices and had to be carried out by my father.

"Oh, you poor thing! You were frail, then?"

"God, yes." I remembered the Communion photos of a sickly child with stick-thin legs. "The nun who was teaching me used to make me bring an egg to school and swallow it down raw mid-morning in front of the whole class. Of course, I loved being the martyr."

Their laughing faces shone red through the mist.

"But sure raw white of egg is toxic!" said Buck Teeth.

"Yeah, but Mother Francis Xavier didn't know that."

"You're a great girl anyway!" said the red-haired one.

"We'll leave you to it," said the other as they pulled away from me in their sturdy brogues.

My second great love – appropriately at puberty – had been the teenage Saint Dominic Savio. He had died heroically of consumption at the age of fifteen. That didn't exactly break the pattern.

I began to pray, reciting the *Hail Mary* like a mantra. It worked, focusing the concentration needed to seek out foothold after foothold, to keep balance when a stone shifted underfoot or a step proved painful. The prayer ebbed and flowed over the surface of my mind while my eyes sought out the best stones and my feet followed through. *Holy Mary, Mother of God, pray for us sinners, now and at the hour of our death. Amen.* What was I praying for? Enlightenment. And rescue. Black Crowes. A Rescue Remedy. I wanted Africa back.

I passed a stout old man in a dark overcoat who was climbing with a staff in each hand, painfully slowly.

Doing without the Walkman was fasting in earnest.

But I loved the Coca-Cola stand. How did Lugh feel about that? Did he move with the times? Libations in coke?

Some time later I overtook a bearded man with a tasselled woolly cap and a guide dog, feeling his way with a white stick, a small straggly-haired woman as his companion.

I tried to get my grip on the *Hail Mary* again but the mountain slid away and there was Amodi, vivid against the background of sand, with his glossy braids and severely beautiful profile, Coca-Cola bottle upended, draining the last drop with the gusto only a Saharan thirst could produce. I wound on rapidly. Another shot. And another. He laughed at me, bottle raised, the logo clear. Would Coca-Cola pay a fortune for this? The Real Thing with sand and headlice on it?

Yes. The desert dotted with coke stands, the sooner the better. And there, right in the heart of the Sahara, right next door to Charles de Foucauld's hermitage and working on the same basic principle, Michael Jackson's Neverland with free popcorn and carousel rides and "My Favourite Things" piped by gnomes in rock gardens.

It would be nice for the kids – a pleasant change from hunger and dying of German measles.

And I preferred it to the blood and the machineguns. The African night throbbed around me like a pulse and blood slid blackly over my forearm in the moonlight as I held the woman again, the mangled baby between us.

I shook my head angrily, rejecting it. That must always be kept at bay. *Hail Mary, Full of Grace!* I muttered savagely.

"Well, I see it as a kind of Noah's Ark!" Prince Philip in his snotty-nosed voice when he had come to establish that animal sanctuary up in the Aïr mountains.

What did he mean? That everything else would be engulfed in sand and hunger? Leaving only the chosen few animals in his sanctuary?

Smug bastard. That was me and my child he was talking about!

Now I was tiring badly. My leg-muscles were starting to tremble. Surely this rise must be the top of the mountain? Where was the scree that the guy had talked about? I crested the rise and there it was, swathed in mist. Like a medieval vision of hell – a huge cone of jagged pieces of rock – dotted by toiling figures struggling to keep their balance as the slabs of rock slipped and slid beneath their feet. Arms flailed outwards for balance or formed chains of support with others. I spotted the woman with the kids halfway up – madness! To bring children up here! But I had seen others. As I watched, a headscarved old woman, rosary wound around her fist, fell on the rocks in a jumble of matchstick limbs. Christ, where did that energy come from? It wasn't a natural strength that drove such a frail old creature up this mountain. Far above, a rearguard Teutonic cameraman was facing downwards, straddled legs and phallic lens making him look like a gigantic Norse god about to urinate on us all.

I heard Maeve's voice, vibrant over the phone from London: "Ellie! You've been climbing Croagh Patricks all your life! What d'yeh want to climb another one for?"

It began to rain again.

I climbed.

*Cork City, Ireland*

It had been a cold, bright day in January. There was even some snow on the ground, the usual meagre Irish two inches. It was still freezing hard. I had come through the university gates and turned right to walk to the corner shop. I had been wearing the tomato-red flared trousers I had bought in Italy – desperate colour, must have been a bargain – and a knee-length coat – green, it would have been green, I always wore green then. Trudging along with my head down, clutching the books and folders to my chest (one of the books was TE Lawrence's *Seven Pillars of Wisdom*, the 700-odd dense pages of which I was doggedly ploughing through), enjoying the way my shoes were slipping from my heels despite the thick socks – that meant my diet was working.

I would have been going to the shop to buy chocolate, to which I was addicted.

Lectures had been cancelled that day because of the weather. So the twenty-mile bus-ride to the city had been a *turus in aisce* – a useless trip. But I hadn't left home for the lectures – it was for the lure of being free – and yes, I hardly remember but no doubt there was some passionate infatuation in progress.

He mustn't have showed because when I went to the shop I know I intended to go to earth in my aunt's little house nearby. I would study and have the pleasures of solitude, coffee, cream cakes, hard cheese, Agatha Christie and the electric fire on full blast – I had many addictions in

17

hose days. Never alcohol, though. I used to drink heavily all right but in pubs. And no grass, I didn't smoke.

The shop was on the corner of a little crossroads but built back from the road so there was a small concrete railed area outside.

A girl was moving about there when I reached it. She was a familiar enough figure, a rough young creature of about fourteen years old, always moving about the neighbourhood like a wild young animal. What drew my attention on this particular morning were her bare legs, mottled blue and white with the cold. Her bare feet were thrust into broken old shoes. She wore a blue dress of some heavy material, well above her knees and short in the arms. She had no coat. She was strongly built, fleshy, freckled, with hair which might have been red-gold under the dirt.

"Gi'us sometin'," she whined. She had an old cardboard box on a string and she moved about restlessly, pulling it over the frozen ground.

I passed her, giving her a wide berth and went quickly into the shop. But, as I stood gazing at the rows of chocolate bars on the counter, I felt a familiar pity wringing my heart. I flushed and my heart began to pound. It was an unmistakable challenge. Images of Francis and Clare of Assisi superimposed themselves on the array of chocolate, heroic figures in a landscape where the Italian light and their inner joy were one and the same. Behind me the girl bounded into the shop, the cardboard box banging behind her.

"Get out of here, girl, out! I've told you we've nothing here for you!" shrilled the hard-faced woman behind the counter. "Go on, now, out! And don't let me see you putting a foot inside this shop again!"

The girl banged the box about sullenly but obeyed. I felt a trembling starting inside me. I hovered over the counter, trying to choose between a Dairy Milk and a Whole Nut – they were such different experiences and I loved both. I wanted both. My mind raced on another level: I must buy something for the girl. I must make a gesture, however feeble. Francis would have stripped off his coat and put it around the mottled shoulders. Francis would have taken the shoes off his feet, given them to the girl and gone home barefoot on the icy ground. Did it snow in Umbria? Francis would have shamed the bitterly-complacent shopkeeper, blinded her with an action of great love.

The woman in question was eyeing me suspiciously, on guard against student pilfering. I gave up on the chocolate and hurriedly bought an iced bun. The woman handed over the change, unsmiling. *A nation of shopkeepers . . . fumble in a greasy till and add the halfpence to the pence and prayer to shivering prayer until you have dried the marrow from . . .* the bone? The soul?

"Will that be all?" asked the shopkeeper sharply.

"Just a minute . . . " I mumbled. What should I buy for the girl? Vague notions of airmen and chocolate flitted through my brain as I tried to avoid the shopkeeper's cold stare through the butterfly glasses over the pursed lips. A bun? No – something nutritious. An apple? Yes. I bought a green apple – that left a shilling. I'd give her the shilling too – I had my bus ticket to get home on.

Outside, the girl confronted me. "Gi'us sometin' t'buy bread," she whined. "I'm starvin'!"

I held out the apple. The green skin looked fresh and bright.

"I don' wan' dat!" She pulled a grotesque face at the apple.

"Why not?" My voice wobbled. I felt something cold and dark slip into my heart. "You said you were starving!"

"I am so I am!" She stared at her box sullenly as she bounced it on its string.

"So why won't you eat an apple?" I was conscious of having said "an apple" rather than "the apple" or "this apple" and I knew it was because I was now terribly ashamed of the thing in my hand and wanted to disown it. Somewhere in the back of my brain anger was dawning.

"'Tisn't fillin'!"

"Yes, it is." But it wasn't, of course. An apple! Stupid! Foolish! What cold comfort to offer on such a morning!

"'Tisn't fillin'. I wan' t'buy a loaf. A loaf is fillin'." She pulled the box over the ground, moving restlessly and clumsily all the time.

Now I was angry. I had made a fool of myself. I pushed on. "Did you eat this morning?"

"Naw! We're starvin' at home, me an' me brodurs an' me sisturs. An' me mammy has a new baby an she's nuttin' t' feed it wit'."

"How many brothers and sisters do you have?"

"Two brodurs an' t'ree sisturs. An' de baby."

Looking at the girl, at the cold raw flesh on the sturdy bones, I had a sense of revulsion. I felt sick. That's what we all were when stripped of pretence. Animal flesh defenceless against pain. I averted my eyes from the girl's body and tried to look her in the eye. But the girl, I then realised, had never looked me in the face from the start. She had been swinging her head from side to side following the movements of her box and making her answers as if she were addressing the box or the ground. Her eyes were a very pale washed-out blue – as if the cold had touched the eyes as well.

"Haven't you got any stockings?"

"Naw! Me sistur took 'um."

I didn't know what to do to rescue my dignity. A remnant of pride made it difficult to offer the shilling after the refusal of the apple. But I couldn't just walk away defeated.

I held the apple out again. "Why won't you take it? 'Tis better than nothing, isn't it?"

"I d'wan' it."

Defeated, I took the shilling from my pocket. "Here, then."

She snatched it. "Gi'us some more! 'Tisn't enough t'buy bread!"

"Well, I haven't any more."

"Gi'us some more an' I'll say a prayer for ya!"

I made to walk past but she stepped backwards and blocked the way out of the railed area. I stopped. The ground was too icy and treacherous to make any vigorous attempt to get past.

The sharp voice of the shopkeeper cut in from behind me. "Don't be encouraging her!" She had come to the door, thin and angular in her apron, teeth falsely regular between the thin lips, hair respectably permed, feet respectably clad in nylon stockings and high heels, even on this coldest day of the year. "We've had enough trouble with her, day in day out!"

The girl fell back a little, stepping outside the railings. I stood there, angry and belittled by the shopkeeper's dismissal.

"Gi'us some more an' I'll say a prayer for ya!" whined the girl with a little less confidence.

"I don't have any more!" I stepped out onto the road, slipped, recovered, and hobbled back onto the icy pavement beyond the girl, walking off in my too-loose shoes, muscles tensed against skidding. I watched myself in my mind's eye, a ridiculous figure. Then I heard the girl's cardboard box slithering along behind her.

"I'll say a prayer for ya! Gi'us some more t'buy bread."

I walked as fast as I dared, heels slipping in the loose shoes. Behind, the box began to bang-bang against the railings of the houses. Across the road was the Convent of the Poor Clares. I thought of their bare frozen feet with envy. The heroic choice. Behind their wall, they were one with the girl with the mottled legs. God! If I had a fraction of their faith I'd gladly join them tomorrow!

Past the university gates again and along the stone wall that separated it from the world. The girl didn't leave me.

Then, just as I turned right and up the little hill that led to the haven of my aunt's house, the girl bounded in front of me and blocked my way.

"I won' let ya go! Gi'me sometin'!"

My heart was hammering. "I don't have any more . . . " My voice was thin in my throat.

Suddenly she grabbed. The fragile chain of the cheap necklace round my neck snapped and the girl held it, with its tiny imitation pearls and cheap gilt medallions, in her fist. "There now. I won' gi' it t'ya!" And now, at last, her eyes were fixed on my face.

"OK. Keep it then. I don't care." But I did care for my bit of cheap finery.

It was a violation. Fear crowded out anger.

"I'm goin' ta keep it unless ya gi' me money."

"Keep it." I walked past her.

She thrust herself in front of me again. Her hand was raised and in it was a large stone. "I'll break yer head wi' dis if ya don' gi' me sometin'!" She made a threatening gesture with the stone.

I managed not to flinch but stood rooted in appalling helplessness. An image of my aunt's little house, small electric bars glowing, kettle steaming on the gas-stove slid into my mind.

Footsteps sounded on the frozen footpath, light but distinct.

A little old woman came down the path, wearing a black coat and a black hat with a net over her forehead. She carried a shopping-bag and a large handbag over one arm. She drew level and stopped, staring at the girl who had hidden the stone in the folds of her skirt.

"What's the matter here?" she asked sharply, in a high but vigorous Cork sing-song.

"She's threatening to hit me with a stone to make me give her money!" My voice trembled. "And she's taken my necklace . . . "

The girl had actually dropped it. It lay, broken and cheap, on the ground near her feet. I stooped and picked it up. It shamed me.

"Aren't you the saucy girl!" cried the little woman stridently. She faced up to the girl like an angry little bird. The top of her hat came nowhere near my shoulder. She shook a black glove in the girl's face. "Who d'yeh think yeh are! Go on away out of here now, before we call the police on yeh!"

I had already moved away. I began to walk up the hill. Halfway up I stopped and looked back. The little woman, looking half the size of the solid girl, was still talking vigorously with her head thrown back to look up at the sullen fleshy face. The girl's hand was still hidden in the folds of her dress. Neither of them looked after me.

I remember all that but I can't remember why I walked away. I remember that when I got to my aunt's house I went in and locked the door and sat down in the little kitchen and put my books down and sat, trembling and crying, for a long time. But I can't remember what exactly I was feeling – whether shame or anger or humiliation or despair or pity.

I find that strange, to remember every detail except that.

That, and why I walked away.

I did eventually finish *Seven Pillars of Wisdom* but I didn't join the Poor Clares. I like to keep my feet warm in winter. In Africa, of course, it was bare feet in rubber sandals for many a year.

# Chapter 1

*Zaria, Northern Nigeria*

While the sun set I felt a longing so great that the
fading light seemed to tremble with energy as if he
must suddenly materialise and stand before me. I gazed from
the verandah and the whole landscape seemed caught in a
tension of expectancy. There was the road to the north, the

road we had taken together, leading out of the grasslands and into the desert. White and blue, the robes of homegoing men on bicycles gleamed phosphorescent. In one corner of my mind, far from the anguish, a lens-shutter clicked open and shut.

I stared at the road and my mind sped along it, following the great sweeping lengths of it up to the border and beyond, far beyond, to where the leather tents sprawled in the sand. Darkness fell with African abruptness and still I sat, drinking my gin, now staring up at the stars. They were brighter where he was. I shut my eyes and imagined it: cool water at the tent door – sand, straw mat and back muscles lean into each other – the eyes look up to brightness and darkness.

Four months ago I had left him there in the desert before driving back to Zaria and flying home to Ireland on leave. I had been back at work for six weeks now. He had promised he would be here. But there was no sign of him, no news.

I was longing for *harmattan* – the dryness, the cold in the mornings, the dust flung against the sun, all omens of the Christmas break from teaching that would free me to go north.

A dull ache of disappointment accompanied me these days. I had come back from leave full of a nervous joy. I had decided. I wanted a child. Marriage or no, I would not be denied that. I had waited long enough and he would never be able to marry me. Marriage was fantasy; a child could be real. A child could be frighteningly real, the point where fantasy crossed with reality, where the word and the will was made flesh.

I was twenty-nine years old.

But Amodi had not come back. I found my house dust-laden, my bush-dog running wild and neglected, all my precious Tuareg knives and silver and leather pieces stolen – by robbers, my young Haruna said – Haruna whose job it was to guard the house and feed the dog in my absence. I wondered.

I was nervous with longing. Every morning I gazed at the road across the empty grass as if the intensity of my gaze could bring Amodi into being, as if the lithe golden frame, the heavy blue-black plaited hair, the almond eyes would shimmer like a shadow in sunlit water and then flare into clarity and focus.

But my will wasn't strong enough. There was nothing to see but braying buses. Yellow taxis. Delusive voices. Imaginings.

What to do?

Lassitude, a great word that. The air still held some of the heavy softness of the rainy season. I was reaching for the gin bottle again, too lazy to go look for tonic and ice, when a car engine throbbed. Headlights swung a lazy arc across the verandah and a car stopped in the space before my bungalow. My Land Cruiser had survived a trip to Kano, returning safely with the American who had borrowed it.

Craig came briskly up the steps, a wide grin on his face. I liked Craig enormously: his openness to experience, his democratic attitudes, his innocent assumption that despite all it was still the best of all possible worlds. He was blond, blue-eyed, tanned, white-toothed, wiry. Californian, what else? He was now a lecturer in Linguistics but he had earned his stripes in the Peace Corps, living hard and poor in the villages down south. Tonight he was wearing semitraditional garb – cut-off denims and a woven black and blue striped Fulani shirt, open down the sides. He was carrying a bottle of wine. Booty from Kano.

"We match," I said nodding down at my dark-blue cotton wrapper and loose black Tuareg shirt – open-sided too but wide enough to fall to my wrists at the sides.

"I know we match," he said, kissing me. His mouth opened as he did and it began to turn into a wet kiss.

So he'd made up his mind to push his luck tonight.

I had lost the art of kissing with the mouth. The Tuareg didn't do it really.

I pulled away, a little abruptly. I wasn't ready for this. He had been ready since I'd met him nine months before.

"Thought you might like to go to the bar to dance afterwards," he said.

"After what?"

"After we drink the wine."

"OK." I went and brought some glasses, candles and mosquito coils.

Gin and wine, not good. I lit the candles, the straight plain household ones we used constantly because NEPA was forever cutting our electricity.

I watched him as he set up the coils at our feet, dark-blond hair springy and vital, lean calves with dark-gold hair. He was a very sexy man. He was also an available man. Open and ready for that easy Californian sexual companionship. How bad? as we said back home in Cork. I was always so bloody perverse, never taking what was on offer, always wanting the thing just out of reach.

"Where's Haruna?" he asked as he settled in one of the wooden-slatted garden chairs.

"Gone to his parents' quarters tonight at the Police Gate. It's a family baptism." I shouldn't have told him. Haruna was a handy and very willing chaperon. He was fifteen years old now and had lived with me since he was ten – packing his few things and arriving at my door, a black-skinned kid with Bambi eyes, armed with a glower, an extraordinary buck-toothed grin and pidgin English, announcing he had come to live with me and cook for me. His father, a Christian from the Jos Plateau, was a cook in the university. Haruna had continued to go to school, though I soon discovered that his notion of reading was to memorise by rote what was on the page, with only the foggiest idea of what the symbols meant. He still couldn't read but now he spoke confident English with a pronounced sing-song Cork inflection – or so my friends told me – I couldn't hear it. The jury was out on whether his brand of extravagant humour was also Cork or all his own.

Craig handed me my glass – the wine was a Bordeaux – and we sat drinking, talking about his trip while my mind raced.

"So, no Haruna . . . and where's Ataka?" he asked, eyebrow and mouth twisting in self-irony.

I laughed ruefully. "There's no one here. Ataka's gone courting – over in the main campus. I guess he'll be back later – maybe."

Ataka was a young Tuareg silversmith, one of the Inaden caste of craftspeople, who had taken up residence in my house. Like Haruna before him, it had been his idea.

Craig laughed softly. He sat at ease – leather sandals thrown off, dusty feet drawn up on the wooden-slatted garden chair. At ease, but I could feel his resolve. The whiteness of his neat teeth irritated me.

As did his assumption that because my lover was a bushman he could be discounted – I couldn't really be serious, could I?

In fact, the whole white community made the same assumption. *Let's ignore such a blatant indiscretion until the poor girl comes to her senses, shall we?* While they gossiped with glee behind my back.

The black reaction was more complex, more hostile.

Somewhere three-quarter-way through the bottle I began to think: why not? Maybe I should? Maybe I should try to break out of this Tuareg addiction of mine? And all the pain it brought with it? Could I?

Had I the humour or the strength – or the sobriety – tonight to hold out against Craig? I had begun to feel a fool, always pleading this absent great love of mine as my excuse for rejecting him.

"It's getting late," he said. A hesitation. "Could I shower? Need to wash off all this dust from the road."

"OK. I must too. You go first. But we must finish the wine."

"Let's finish it in the shower . . . " he grinned.

I laughed to cover my unease and in a hair's breadth of time thought: go straight to it or you'll flounder.

He took a candle and the wine into the bathroom. I followed nervously with the glasses.

I knew already it wasn't going to work. I couldn't share his mood and felt his initial gaiety slip away like the water swirling down the drain as we emptied the bath – constantly kept full as not a day passed without the water being cut off for a period. We stripped and stepped into the bath and covertly I checked out his penis – so that was where he got his air of confident sexuality – in its semi-erect state it looked huge on his slim frame. We washed, very respectably, he with calabashes of water from the storage bucket, me under the tap of the hot-water heater. "Shower" was a misnomer – the colonial British had never heard of the things. I thought wryly of Travis McGee's "enormous shower-stall" on the Busted Flush as, chastely, we washed each other's backs. I'm no good at this sort of thing, I thought. I need to be in love. I want Amodi. Pain wrenched about my heart. I stepped out and wound a towel modestly about my waist, ill at ease and still trying to disguise it. Fuck. I sat on the edge of the bath. Trying to keep up with a Californian, I thought with a private grimace. Here I was a stranger in a strange country. In a goatskin tent I had been myself and at home.

He turned to me naked and bent to kiss my lips, his erection prodding my thigh. I stood up and went into his arms, more out of embarrassment than anything else. I didn't want to kiss. I turned my head to one side and saw us embracing in the mirror above the sink, my paler face on his brown shoulder. And next to the mirror the calendar, with its pictures of gaudy traditional dancers, day after day crossed out in red, counting the days to Amodi's return.

We lay on the hard cool tiles of the bathroom floor and coupled. He was very good but I didn't come and when he did, it was with a wild prolonged cry which aroused only a faint repugnance and contempt in me.

Later we danced in the village, in the open courtyard of the bar, on a cement floor glossy from the friction of many feet over the years. Great bottles of Nigerian beer stood on the tables around, the green glass glinting. The music was modern Nigerian dance music – Yoruba, probably, from the south. It flowed cool and powerful, layer upon layer, like the great river Niger itself: endless, seething on the surface, relentlessly calm in its depths. The river of life. It lifted me out of myself, my misery. Nothing mattered after all but to be borne along by the current. I let the music take me and on that journey I was not alone. I was part of a whole, together with my fellow-dancers and this man who was now my lover.

"I'm happy!" I thought exultingly and threw back my head and in that moment saw the stars set in blackness above me. The noise and the movement fell away and I was drawn upwards into the stillness of the night sky. I tasted all the bitterness of loss and betrayal.

# Chapter 2

The next morning before seven I was woken by a knocking at the French door of my bedroom. My heart hammered awake and my first thought, sending me trembling to the window, was of Amodi. I parted a curtain and, with the now familiar stab of disappointment, saw a slim compact red-haired figure standing on the porch – my friend Michael, his pea-green Peugeot parked outside.

Something about his stance told me it was news, bad

news – but of what? His Sideka, most likely – I wasn't the only one waiting day by day.

But it could be news of Amodi. Or Haruna who hadn't come home yet – an accident, a fight? Or – the constant fear – some political change that meant we were all to be deported or worse . . . was there a worse?

If he'd come just to borrow my typewriter, to do a last-minute write-up for a nine o'clock History lecture, I'd gut him. He was looking sharp, dressed "formally" in a dark-green short-sleeved shirt and light trousers – heading for classes definitely.

Memories of last night's pleasure stirred and shot through my anxiety as I fastened a wrapper around my waist with fingers slick with sweat and pulled a shirt on. I had sent Craig home in the early hours, pleading the need to sleep.

I opened the door to a nervous smile from Mike – though Mike's smile was nervous at the best of times.

"Hi – sorry to wake you," he said and he cleared his throat.

"Oh, if it wasn't you 'twould be Haruna or any one of a dozen Buzus," I said, using the local and derogatory word for the Tuareg, a word originally applied only to Tuareg slaves.

I went back in and flung myself into an armchair, tension simmering under the surface like the heat of the day waiting to pounce.

He sat opposite on the extreme edge of a chair, white-faced, and fixed his grey-green eyes on mine. His light-red hair was dank from the shower and slicked back, waves tamed for a brief while. The paleness of his face made his freckles show through the tan. He was Irish-American and looked it. Boston.

"I went by the building-site last night," he said.

*Looking for news of Sideka . . .*

"They had some bad news . . . "

*Tell me.*

"They told me your friend – "

*Amodi! A lurch of the stomach.*

" – Yusuf was in a bus accident yesterday morning. On the road from Kaduna."

*Not Amodi.*

I waited. I didn't really have to ask. The buses were transport vans, metal eggshells that crushed everyone when they flipped off the road – in an accident everyone died.

"I'm sorry." He licked lips that were almost as pale as his face. He was still looking intently at me. "He's dead."

I stared and didn't speak.

Why was he trembling like that? Death was all around us.

"Some of his friends went to Kaduna to identify the body." He swallowed nervously, started to speak, then swallowed again.

I concentrated on the movement of his throat. Was that an involuntary movement? Or a pseudo-empathetic thing?

"They went with that American, his *maigida* – what's his name – Mitch – he was there last night, he called by while I was there." Now he looked down at his hands as if surprised to see them there. He began to squeeze the knuckles of one hand rhythmically and then the other, in an odd sort of milking motion. "Apparently Mitch's wife is taking it very badly." He glanced up at me again. "How long had he been their nightwatchman? Four years? Since you first came?"

"Nearly five."

"They sure loved the guy."

"He was very loveable," I said. Thinking of how his eyes used to glint and shine with fun and pleasure, even just greeting a stranger – like me.

Mike was studying his hands again, stretching out the fingers.

"What was he doing in Kaduna?" The false coldness of my voice distressed me. *God damn it*. Why, in crisis, did I always retreat into a remote emotionless place? "He should have been on his way north to Niger."

"Someone there owed him money . . . "

"So did he get it?" I knew the answer.

"Well – there was nothing on him anyway – just a couple of naira."

Passing predators – probably the police – would have scooped it up.

"Did he have all his savings on him?" I asked.

"No – luckily – " he grimaced on the word, flushing, "he left his money with the Americans – he was to collect it on his way back. They have his things – there's his ID card and sword and some other stuff."

He fell silent.

I said nothing.

Then he said: "They want to see you – Mitch and Nancy. Mitch asked me to let you know . . . before you heard it from the Tuaregs."

I put my elbows on my knees and hid my face in my hands. No tears. Well, it wasn't Amodi.

We sat there in silence.

"Sorry, Ellen," he said at last.

"Yeah."

He cleared his throat. "Do you want me to go with you to the house?"

He knew, of course, that the gentle beautiful Yusuf had at one time been more than a friend to me. No one else knew that. But Mike and myself always went in for the late-night drunken confessions.

"No, I'll be fine."

⚜⚜⚜⚜⚜

I lay on my bed, eyes closed, clutching my cassette-player to my heart . . .

*The young women of "America" don't drink,*
*Cow's milk is no longer stored in vessels.*
*They stand at alms-giving places.*
*Tailor, they're begging you!*
*Please, tailor, have a close look at them –*

Yusuf's voice with its clear, high, almost yodelling timbre, filled the room with the lament for his people . . .

Who had backed him the night I recorded this? Was that Ilyas's voice? Sideka's?

*The beautiful ones are all burnt,*
*Their long hair is no longer buttered,*
*They only water American powdered milk and drink it.*
*These sisters live in misery.*
*There are no cattle to catch*
*For they have, like their mothers, all vanished too.*
*But only last year, on moving camp for salt*
*At Agayya, they were all queens, young men and women*

*Sinning and making merry.*

I wouldn't normally have understood such a song with its poetic twists of syntax but this one I knew by heart and had translated it into English.

*May Allah protect me against nightwatching*
*For the most monstrous pagan man*
*Who eats the impure meat of pigs and dogs,*
*Has turned donkeymeat into goatmeat*
*And Sunday into Friday.*
*He owns houses full of beer that he also drinks*
*And yet they call him Alhaji*
*Because he has motor-cars, money, labourers and watchmen.*
*May an abscess of the neck get you*
*To teach your father that you're a dog!*
*I trust in Him who has goats, has Niger,*
*Has taken Diori out*
*And put in Kountche,*
*Has wiped out that one's numerous cattle*
*And left the Tuareg so destitute*
*They began to be watchmen.*

A murmur of guttural Tamajegh. A laugh. Then silence. I pressed *stop*.

In the evening I went and Nancy showed me his few things – his ID card, blanket, sword, tea-making gear, glossy leather whip, his expensive *ilesham* turban recently bought from Kano to show off on his up-coming trip home, the two small cotton dresses for his little girls, the thick bale of soft black heavy cotton for Yassine his wife.

I let Nancy cry in my arms as we sat on their living-room sofa among their collection of African artefacts. It seemed to me like a luxury I couldn't afford – to cry. How could love and grief be so simple and easy for her?

"Nancy, did you actually see him?" I didn't really want to hear but I had to ask, for her.

"No," she gulped into my shoulder. "They said he . . . that it would be too bad . . . Mitch saw him . . . "

Suddenly, I wanted to tell her. In a way, it was a kind of spite. A jealousy that she, as his employer, should claim the right to cry, through the odd bottle of coke handed out through the kitchen door, through the pittance paid out for the glamorous privilege of having a veiled warrior, equipped with whip and sword, living on a mat outside their house to guard it. A handy satisfying right-to-your-door way of dispensing drought relief.

This was viciously unfair but I was possessed of an instinct I could hardly control – a jealous instinct, yes. That she and Mitch, as *uwargida* and *maigida*, mistress and master, could claim that bond with him. While I – what claim had I?

It would be easy: *Nancy, did you know? About Yusuf – and me?*

She lifted her head from my shoulder and gazed at me with her red-rimmed eyes. It was almost as if I had spoken aloud. Then she sat back and reached for a piece of cheap rough Nigerian toilet tissue. I watched her blow her reddened nose and still wanted to say something. She pushed her blonde hair, dark with sweat, back behind her ears.

*Say it!* It would be easy. I could hear myself tell her, deliberately letting my voice tremble to ensure sympathy and leniency: *Yusuf and me – we were lovers, you know. We used to make love – brief couplings, granted – on the mat outside your back door . . .*

"Oh God . . . " Her voice was cracked and nasal from crying. She blew her nose again. "I – " She bit her lip and the tears started to flow again. "I can't bear to think of his wife and children," she sobbed.

His wife and children. Yassine and the little girls. They always seemed so distant in the almost mythical desert. But he loved them, was full of pride in them. Told me often how beautiful she was. We had carried our little affair lightly. We knew it was just play.

I picked up the *ilesham* from the pathetic pile, the burnished purple-copper sheen of the dye beaten into it coming off on my hands.

The everyday dark-blue turban – the *tagilmoust* – was steeped in indigo too but the *ilesham* was produced by a lengthy process which gave it its metallic glitter.

"He never got to wear it," she said, sniffling. "They buried him in his ordinary turban."

Probably opened out the whole eight yards of it and used it as a shroud.

I picked up the folded cream blanket – also streaked with the everyday blue of indigo from his skin and headdress – and laid it on my lap. I had bought it for him. It was made of two wide strips of thick loosely-woven cotton that had originally been only roughly attached. I ran a fingernail down the ridge of the seam where the strips were joined, sewn expertly in thick black thread by Yusuf himself. I smiled. The Tuareg had no sexist attitudes to sewing.

I remembered the first time I laid eyes on him – dream-come-true time. In one fell swoop I'd followed the Yellow Brick Road and been to see the Wizard.

I laughed shakily. "I'm remembering the morning of the light-bulb," I said to her.

She laughed now too, wiping her nose with the flat of her hand.

I turned my head and looked out through the window and mosquito-netting. "Stepping out on your verandah that first morning after I arrived – was it the first morning?"

"Yes, it was," she said, still smiling.

"And seeing Yusuf screwing in that lightbulb in the porch with Mohomed holding the chair . . . " A Laurel and Hardy scenario; but to me the two lean golden figures had stepped right out of David Lean's *Lawrence of Arabia*. "I couldn't believe it."

I had wanted to go to Saudi and live in the desert with the Bedouin.

Instead, the desert had come to me.

I smiled at Nancy and said, as I had often said to her before, "I had forgotten about the Sahara. Somehow it didn't figure, big as it was."

Her eyes were shining through tears and she bit her full lips as they trembled in a smile.

I had got a job in Zaria and come to Black Africa. But so had the desert nomads when the droughts of the early seventies wiped out their herds of camels and goats. Over the northern border straggled groups of turbaned men armed with swords, daggers and whips, who worked exclusively as security guards and nightwatchmen: the People of the Veil, the fearsome Blue Men who had raided and ruled the Sahara for centuries – now destitute, with nature and the modern nation-state joining forces against them.

That morning, mesmerised, I stepped up close to Yusuf and Mohomed and, as they greeted me smilingly with the graceful formal hand to the heart, I smelt for the first time that intoxicating musky blend of heavy oil-based perfume, tobacco, indigo dye and sweat on warm skin. They greeted me "smilingly", I say – but the folds of their turbans were drawn up over mouths and noses and I saw only dark almond eyes glinting in the slit below the heavy twists of blue-black cloth around their heads.

I was hooked.

I fell instantly in love – not just with Yusuf but with the whole damn culture.

I began to sit with them on their mats outside people's houses and at various building-sites in the university, learning to know them. I began with sign language, then tried to learn Tamajegh by writing it down word by word in Tifenagh, the script they had inherited from the ancient Phoenicians. But soon I lapsed into learning Hausa, the local language, an easier option than the vigorous and difficult Tamajegh.

I couldn't understand their fearsome, sometimes gruesome, reputation. They were full of warmth and grace and talk and play. With Yusuf, play soon moved on to sexual play and when I got my own bungalow he continued to visit me.

Maybe it was just the veil that had made them bogeymen. But for me the dark eyes glinted with fun and affection through the slits of their turbans. Yet they called themselves, not Tuareg which was the Arab name for them, but *Kel Tamajegh* – the people who raid – and had been the scourge of the Sahara for centuries, raiding or exacting protection money from caravans or swooping down like vultures on villages on the southern fringes of the desert, carrying off their inhabitants into slavery. The French had only managed to subdue them as late as 1902 when a detachment of ninety Arab *meharistes* with superior modern firepower had slaughtered one hundred and fifty warriors in southern Algeria.

"Ellen?" said Nancy.

"Yes?"

She was snuffling into her tissue but now more composed. "Mitch and I wanted to ask a favour of you . . . "

"Yes?" I said more warily.

"Wait . . . " She got up and padded barefoot over the tiled floor out of the room.

I picked up his green university card with the ABU emblem and opened it to his photograph inside – taken of course without his customary headdress. He had cut his plaits off before taking this photo and his thick dark hair stood up untidily around his head. The dark stain of the indigo dye around the neck of his white gown was clear. It was so pathetic – this displaced person who should never have been on one of those lethal buses on the Kaduna road to be smashed and shattered – or worse, to bleed to death at the side of the road as he probably did.

Nancy came back with an envelope in her hand. She laid it on the blanket on my lap.

I looked inside. It was a thick wad of naira notes. I looked up questioningly.

She sat, tucking one plump bare leg under her, now in control again. "His savings and wages, with some extra. I had been keeping them for him . . ." She hesitated.

"What do you want me to do with it?" I asked.

"Well, it seems like a lot to ask – but Mitch and I – we're afraid to trust anyone with it. We want it to reach his wife and kids safely . . . so we wondered if you could take it to Niger yourself?"

# Chapter 3

I drove home with my mind racing. Nancy's request was like a shot of whiskey to an alcoholic. Niger was like a fever in my blood and the mere suggestion I should go there immediately had me shaking. Two days and my agony of waiting could be over . . . I could be with Amodi.

Could I make a case to persuade the department to let me go? Now, mid-term, before the Christmas break?

It was by now dark but my lights picked out the green Peugeot approaching and I braked instinctively.

Mike pulled up across the road and leaned out. "Like a drink at the Club?" he called, a bleak invitation.

I signed yes.

We drove to the Samaru Club – somewhere along the way NEPA went on the blink and by the time we got there the club was in darkness. A few candles glimmered on the tables and a gas camping-lamp was set up on the bar.

Mike slumped in his chair, exhausted. "Ah, yes, we need this," he said as we sipped the warm beer, surveying the dismal scene, with the mosquitos taking their first nips from our ankles. He was wearing jeans, the best protection, but with open leather sandals. "What would we do without this little dollop of luxury?"

I grinned but I was too wound up to lapse into the flights of fancy that usually served us as conversation. "I've just come from Yusuf's place. I collected his stuff. She gave me his money too. Four hundred naira. With a blow-up beachball and a stuffed toy."

He stared, startled. "What for?"

"They want me to take them north – to find his wife and kids."

"That's a cool order."

"I don't think they have the foggiest notion what they're asking. But I didn't enlighten her."

"Why don't they give them to one of the guys – his friends or cousins?"

"Don't trust them." Right, too.

He pulled a face and nodded. "Where are they? His wife and kids?"

"They're in In-Gall – west of Agadez."

"Wasn't he from Tchin Tabaraden?"

"Yeah, but they're settled in In-Gall at the moment – as far as I know."

"Will you go?"

"How can I? Mid-term?"

He fell silent.

What if I went? I could take Haruna as mechanic and Ilyas, Sideka's older brother, as guide . . . and Ataka had been pining for home . . .

We listened to the mosquitos buzz in the dark. I closed my eyes and visualised the interior of Mike's head – I could hear his thoughts buzz as loud as any cloud of trapped mosquitos.

Into the cloud I dropped the question. "No news of Sideka?" I asked casually.

"No."

A long silence.

"He's very late for school now," I said.

"Yeah. And he knows that. I don't know . . . I think I'd have heard if he was sick . . . " He gave a miserable little shrug and my heart bled for him. He looked so vulnerable sitting there. "If Amodi came, he'd have news of him . . . they might come together."

"I think that is probably what will happen." Sometimes I thought that.

"Anything could have delayed them . . . " he said.

A wedding. A funeral. A fever.

A trip to Libya to join Gaddafi's Tuareg battalion. I shook my head, shaking the thought off.

"I slept with Craig the Californian last night," I said then. "At least, we fucked on the bathroom floor." It was easier to tell if I did it crudely. "Umm – initially."

47

"I don't believe it." His laugh was a little gasp.

"For all the good it did. I'm still desperate for Amodi."

"You're crazy, girl. You and Craig make a great couple. Hell, you have fun together."

I shrugged. I didn't look at him but I could see his head incline in my direction.

"So how was he?" he asked.

"What do you think?"

"Sexy as a tomcat?" He giggled softly.

"Right."

"It shows – he's bursting with it."

"Well, you have him then."

He didn't answer. We were silent.

The warm beer had gone down too easily and fizzily. I took one more slug and my glass was empty.

"Another beer?" he asked then.

I shook my head. "These mosquitos are eating me up."

And still we sat. Soft laughter, a clinking of glasses and some movement from the bar. Otherwise it was just us and the mosquitos.

"So?" he asked eventually. "No hope for Craig then?"

I shook my head ruefully.

"You're fixated," he said.

*And you're a fine one to talk.* "Never denied it."

"How did it happen, actually?"

"What? My fixation? Well . . . " I shrugged.

"No, tell me . . . I know about TE and the Bedouin and all – but what sparked that off to begin with?"

"Oh, God, so many things . . . "

"Tell me one of them," he said lazily. "One I don't know."

I laughed. "Well . . . OK . . . one you don't know . . . that's

48

difficult. OK. When I was about nine my father brought a Spanish sailor home to dinner – " I glanced at him in time to catch his faint smirk. "*No* – not *that* – don't be daft – my father was learning Spanish and we were living in Bantry where Spanish trawlers lined the harbour wall. And he had to go on the boats and trawlers to check – I dunno – "contributions" – whatever that meant – because he was a Social Welfare Officer, a Pensions Officer we used to call it – "

"Yeah – get back to the Spanish sailor."

"Right. Well, he brought this sailor home to dinner. My father was very eccentric for a small-town civil servant – never gave a damn what anyone thought – "

"You must be so unlike him – "

"The sailor's name was Jesus, they told me – I remember we had peas *and* carrots for dinner because when my mother flashed the tins or bunches of carrots or whatever at him, by way of asking him which he wanted, he said 'Bofe'. He was dark and lean and muscular and wearing dark blue trousers and a black shirt. Anyway, before he left he squatted down, embraced and kissed me. I still remember how he smelt – spicy. To this erotic experience I attribute my lifelong fixation on lean, dark exotic men – dressed in dark blue – "

"And preferably squatting – "

"Preferably squatting."

"Ships of the desert?"

"That pass in the night . . . " I grinned. "So here I am . . . my father didn't live long enough to see what he was responsible for . . . "

He looked disconcerted. He took a long pull on the dregs of his beer until the empty glass made a sucking sound.

I watched him out of the corner of my eye, waiting. I had

intended to amuse but he didn't like my story of early sexual programming. Naturally he wouldn't. Maybe he thought I was slyly getting at him?

I made it worse. "Four or five years later I was kissed again – again by a much older man – married. But by that time the nuns had got me in their clutches and I felt violated."

"Washed your mouth out, did you?" he said joylessly.

"I was angry. I was trying to be a saint, you see, and a saint should not be contaminated." Philomena had chosen instead to be shot with arrows, tied to an anchor and thrown off a cliff.

I wanted to say, jocosely, *So what happened to you, buddy? You're not even Irish. What screwed you up so badly?* "Better get back," I said instead.

"Your Haruna called around today," he said abruptly.

"Did he?" Oh? He had made it sound like an extension of the previous subject of conversation.

He was busily picking at his nails. "Mmm. Doesn't he ever get jealous?"

"Jealous?"

"Of Craig, for instance."

"Well, yes, he does – a bit."

"Is it fair to do that to him?"

"Do what to him? I'm not doing anything to him."

"Aren't you?" he countered swiftly. He shot a look at me from under his lashes.

"No, I'm not." I stared back. "What? What do you mean?" He looked into his glass.

"What?" But I knew what that look had said. "What? Do you think I'm having sex with him?"

There was a long pause.

"You do!" I flushed with anger.

He fiddled with his glass, glanced at me, began to say something and thought better of it.

I was too angry to let it pass. Haruna was my child, the teenager I was rearing without the benefit of motherhood. He'd been with me since he was ten. "Well, do you?"

He was now scared of me. Women scared him easily. He must have had a termagant of a mother.

He was sucking from the empty glass again. He put it down and said, quietly, "I'm sorry. I always assumed you were."

"Why the hell would you assume that?" Ask a stupid question . . .

"Sorry," he said. "I just thought you were."

*Besides, what of my relationship with Amodi?* I stood up abruptly, the metal legs of the chair scraping angrily on the concrete floor. "I'm going."

"Ellen!"

I kept going. I couldn't take it tonight. I was filled with a cold rage.

I clambered into the Land Cruiser and pushed the accelerator down recklessly. The car gave a violent jolt and I was thrown forward against the wheel. I had forgotten to release the handbrake. I started up again and drove off shakily.

I saw his headlights behind me. He drew level with me as I pulled up outside my house.

I turned off the engine and sat there. He got out of his car and stood, leaning on the roof of the car, not making any attempt to approach me. The moon was full. White light spilled everywhere.

I sat for a while, cooling off. *Hypocrite*, said a savage little voice in my head. I remembered Haruna's approaches to me, the couple of nights that I had woken to find him in the bed with me, a hand surreptitiously edging under my wrapper. Of course, I had made myself more than clear to him each time in an explosion of violent slapping. But I would never tell anyone of that.

With an effort, I got out and crossed to Michael and we faced each other across the roof of his car.

"Night," he said, with a wisp of a smile.

"Mike," I said, "that was a stupid and insulting thing to say . . . "

He stared. "I didn't intend it to be. I don't see that it is. I'm sorry. And I shouldn't have said it tonight – "

We stood, caught in a web of unspoken things. The silence went on.

I was weary of the fencing. "Mike. I've got to go – to Niger. To find Amodi."

His mouth quivered on a question and he swallowed. Then he said, "Go. I'll do my best to cover for you. Tell you what – go at the weekend – supposedly just to deliver Yusuf's things to somewhere fairly close by, like Tahoua. Come Monday or Tuesday I can pretend I got a message from Niger saying you're sick or the car has broken down. Yeah?"

"Yeah. Jesus, thanks Mike. I just can't bear the waiting – not knowing if he's alive or dead – if he'll ever come back – "

He looked directly at me across the car and on his face I saw a mirror-image of my pain.

Compassion overwhelmed me.

"Mike," I said. "I'll find Sideka for you. I'll bring him back with me."

# Chapter 4

*In-Gall, Niger*

When we were told at the border that the military at Tahoua were not allowing any vehicles to travel north to Tchin Tabaraden and into the desert, I shook with fright. What was going on out there that they should deny access?

Luckily, I had given In-Gall rather than Tchin Tabaraden as our destination and so the border police at Birnin Konni quite cheerfully instructed us to take the long way round, making a huge 1200 kilometre loop east to Zinder, north-west to Agadez and then south-west to the oasis of In-Gall. In-Gall was accessible apparently, Tchin Tabaraden not. Or else, perhaps they trusted that the long haul would discourage us and that we would turn back. They scrutinised Ilyas's ID card which gave Tazerza beyond Tchin Tabaraden as his birth place but handed it back without comment. A teenager didn't merit much concern, I suppose, or else they casually took him for my servant, part of my household.

I was glad we had dropped Ataka off a mile or so before the border – two passengers from Tazerza would have made it awkward. Not having an ID card, Ataka had opted to walk through the bush into Niger rather than run the gauntlet of the police post. We would pick him up on the outskirts of the town . . .

> Sharibu came to the border where the police stopped him,
> He and many friends,
> But he said, "Worthless slave,
> You'll not put Sharibu into prison,"
> And struck him so that his gun fell
> And he had to search about for it on the ground;
> Sharibu went through and left his friends,
> They fired at him but he escaped . . .

No such heroics for Ataka.

We dawdled around the outskirts of Birnin Konni, eyes nervously peeled for Ataka. I sweated against the plastic seats of the Land Cruiser, bit my nails unmercifully and brooded.

The news was ominous, with its undefined threat. The

political situation in the north of Niger was fraught with possibilities of disaster, the whole power-structure being weighted to the south-west. There the capital, Niamey, stood on the banks of the Niger, set squarely in the relatively fertile country populated by Niger's most powerful political group, the Djerma. Along the south of the country was a strip of arid farmland cut through by the *route nationale*, a single ribbon of tarred road heading straight as a die west to east. This was Hausaland; the Hausas were the second most powerful and numerically the strongest group. Beyond that ribbon of road the country stretched hugely north, a great anvil of desert sparsely populated by small nomadic tribes: the Tuareg, the Arabs, the Peuhl and Wodaabe, the Kanuri and others.

There was a sense then in which the north and south of the country were caught in an eternal antagonistic tension, as if there were an invisible tripwire running between them, always threatening and eventually fated to set off a cataclysmic explosion.

"What has happened, Ellen?" Ilyas was at the window, grinning at my preoccupation. He handed me in a tepid bottle of coke and a little enamel plate of dried meat. The chewy meat was peppered and paper-thin, almost transparent in the sun, glowing bright orange-red.

"I'm worried. Maybe we won't be able to get to your place."

"Don't worry," he said in English with a little roll on the r's. "We will go to Agadez and then to In-Gall. From Agadez," he lapsed into Hausa, "we will steal our way until we come to our home." To Tazerza – their *harmattan* dry-season resting-place, some two hundred kilometres west of In-Gall.

"Great," I said. "One thousand five hundred kilometres instead of four hundred and fifty. Terrific." We had already travelled more than five hundred kilometres from Zaria to the border. But Ilyas's optimism cheered me.

I took my camera and plunged it deep into one of my big yellow tins of powdered NIDO milk, for fear that it might be confiscated at one of the many road-blocks. That had happened to me before in Tchin Tabaraden – damned if I'd let it happen again and be robbed once more of my chance to photograph the desert people. Afterwards I marvelled at the risk I actually took, doing that. If they had found it hidden they might have thought I was a spy for Gaddafi's Libya and had me shot at dawn.

An hour passed and then we spotted Ataka sauntering through the bush towards the town, suitcase in hand, with his dyed leather bag of silversmith's tools on his back. When he saw us his face broke into a dazzling smile. Amodi had the most amazing looks, a strong heart-shaped sculptured face with high cheekbones and wide doe-like eyes – all emphasised by hair braided close to his head. It was a look that to my friends' western eyes was androgynous but was tough rather than soft – the look of a young Tracy Chapman or Joan Armatrading. The curved eyelashes made me feel he should star in some Walt Disney movie, maybe even as a cartoon.

He climbed on board and we set out along the ribbon of tarred road leading east. It took us a day to cover the five hundred kilometres to Zinder, speeding recklessly along the *route nationale* between police-posts, three hours to do the one hundred and sixty kilometres on the tarred road to Tanout, and three days – with under-age Haruna at the wheel now that we were out of the reach of the law – to navigate the three hundred kilometres of deeply rutted desert track between Tanout and Agadez.

Haruna had served a hard apprenticeship since the day when he'd first said, "Ellen, let me drive", on a laterite road outside Tahoua in Niger. Twelve years old, he sat in and drove and never looked back nor lost the ecstatic grin that pasted itself across his face that day. So he and I had blundered as rank greenhorns into these desert trips together, originally in a blue VW Beetle, accompanied by various Tuaregs who didn't have a fucking clue and encouraged the lunacy of driving without heavy-duty tyres through sand spiked with huge six-inch thorns. On one insane trip thirteen-year-old Haruna, without even the proper tools, had laboured single-handed, endlessly removing and mending tyres as we progressed. He was something else.

He worked hard at the wheel of the Land Cruiser on the tough road to Agadez. But the kid was born to drive.

So we drove and sweated and burnt and thirsted. Zaria seemed a planet away. Not only did I not worry about how the university was taking my disappearance, I didn't think of it at all. We stopped in Agadez for a day and a night: not to see the landmark mosque with its tall mud minaret or visit the market and bargain for Tuareg swords, but to guzzle tepid Coca-Cola from labouring fridges like ravenous babies at the breast; to buy coffee thick with sweetened condensed milk in glasses; to sit and endlessly make *shayi* – sweet green tea; to buy little cartons of insipid orange juice; to hail the Peuhl women so they could spoon out measures of fermented milk from their huge calabashes. And for me, to surreptitiously drink cool green bottles of *Flag* beer in the little mud-walled hotels. To drink and drink and drink.

In shade. In the shade of tin-roofed shacks, straw-roofed shelters, mud-roofed huts, leather-roofed tents, green-leaved palm-trees. Sweltering, sweat-drenched shade – but shade, out of the cruel eye of the sun.

From Agadez we turned southwest and swayed our way through white sand to In-Gall.

My fears had receded – fears about Amodi, about bearing the bad news of Yusuf, about the ominous news from Tchin Tabaraden – and despite a faint nervous simmering in the blood, I was wild with joy. To travel towards an ever-receding horizon, to be in motion while my soul stretched out to what might be beyond – I could ask for no more. In my visions I'm always climbing a mountain – heaven is the ultimate view from the top.

I had surely caught the bug from my father. He, in the small scope of West Cork, had knocked out enough adventure to infect me for a lifetime. Once we had driven over a mountain in a little beetle VW and, on the other side, asked a local – peaked cap, stick, wellingtons, sheepdog – the way back to Glengarriff or Bantry or Kenmare or wherever we had come from.

After the requisite amount of cap-adjusting, head-scratching, stick-wielding and wellington-shuffling, he answered. "You must go back the way you came."

"No, no – the main road – where's the main road back?"

"Shur, ye came the only road there is!"

"No – we came that way – over the mountain."

"Yerrah, ye couldn't have – no one's been over that track for a hundred years! There was never a motor vehicle on it at all at all!"

And all those trips – over mountains and to visit farmers black with the dirt and up boreens guarded by vicious dogs and over fields where we were chased by bulls – all the trips involved us shoving stones under the wheels to stop the mud-bemired car from plunging over nearby cliffs while my mother cowered by the side of the road – or waiting in the car while my father set off one more time to trudge the miles to the nearest petrol station, gallon in hand. There was never such a man for running out of petrol. I think he did it from a subliminal desire to create drama. I've certainly inherited that one from him.

*Northwest Passage* was one of his favourite books – he most relished the scene where Rogers and his men crawl and stumble starving out of the trackless wilderness – *where the Ammonoosuc ran to join the broad Connecticut* – only to discover a deserted fort and the ghost of a fire and to hear the parting shots of the Rangers as they disappear downriver with all the provisions, abandoning them to their fate.

And, of course, all the war movies and westerns he brought me to – all those cattle drives and barren wastes and tumbling weeds and Cool Clear Water.

Now, as we sucked the petrol up through tubes from our jerrycans I knew who to blame for my excesses.

Way back then, this had become the only way to live.

So at length we came to In-Gall where we stayed in a mud house on the edge of the oasis village. It could have been the set for an overblown clichéd version of *The Desert Song*, more like the European emblem of the desert oasis than the real thing. At night we sat on white sand by a still pool of water while a huge moon sailed through the diamond-encrusted sky. No trace of the *harmattan* yet with its burden of red dust. A clump of palm-trees hung obligingly and picturesquely over the pond.

The snake in Paradise in this case was the drinking water which was laden with salt – Teguidda-n-Tessoumt with its open salt ponds was not far away to the north. I longed for a long pull of Zaria water, laden with microbes and visible filth.

Yassine was everything Yusuf had boasted of. Now I could understand the pride in his eyes, the quiet earnestness of the "beautiful!" gesture of finger through palm. And, yes, I used to be jealous when he did that – somehow the idea of a husband being so openly adoring of a wife seemed strange and enviable. She was a pint-sized Venus, bone-structure strong under features that managed to be classical yet sensuous; yet somehow the overall effect of the plump bare bouncing breasts and curving buttocks on her tiny frame was of a pert prettiness – she was so tiny she hardly came up to my shoulder and I'm not tall. She was, of course, utterly blue from head to toe, her entire gold-brown skin impregnated with indigo dye from her clothes.

As if the total effect weren't fascinating enough, she had a matching accessory – a tiny child, Yusuf's daughter Raechitu, two years old but hardly bigger than a large doll. Raechitu was tiny and perfect – almost. Her thin little frame hadn't a scrap of infant fat but the stomach was round and prominent. The little thing was half-starved, too old to be still almost entirely dependent on her mother's scant supply of milk.

I had seen this so often – the nomads had no notion of how to feed their children on the food of the towns – thinking handfuls of white bread and rice were a substitute for the whole grains and the generous supplies of camel and goat milk that were the lifeblood of the desert.

Her sister Muhane, however, who was about six or seven years old, was healthy and lively – they must have seen better days during her infancy.

We had given Raechitu the orange and white beachball and, when I ventured to give my camera a few outings from its NIDO tin, I took a picture of her holding it, dwarfed by it, small stick arms stretched around it. But the picture pained me. I could only look at her and think: her little body is starving. And: why don't they see it? But perhaps they did: the charms that hung about her tiny frame were reminders of the childhood diseases so likely to kill her – measles, meningitis, pneumonia.

As for the stuffed bear – within two days Yassine had pulled the stuffing out and was using it to wrap and cushion her tea-glasses. I ended up feeling ashamed of our gifts and annoyed at the Americans who had inflicted them on me.

I had given Yassine the money as formally as I could and she had accepted it with dignity – but without thanks – and gravely tied it into the corner of her blue-black veil. Our news had travelled before us somehow and I was spared having to announce Yusuf's death.

On the second day after our arrival I woke up to find an elderly sinewy man and a wrinkled scrap of a woman sitting there staring at me.

"Yusuf," said the old man, pointing at himself, "Aba". He pointed at the woman. "Yusuf . . . Ana."

It was Yusuf's father and mother.

The extent of the catastrophe hit me in one instant. I had given all the money to Yassine. No one had told me his parents were in In-Gall.

I had to rustle up a little money of my own to give them and get Ilyas to interpret for me, explaining why it was so little.

They seemed peeved with Yassine, to say the least. I suspected there might be some deeper division.

It was an uneasy encounter. There were a few tears from the mother but no great scenes of distress or grief. Dignity was all. And patience.

Yassine, in fact, seemed in good enough form. Our presence, of course, made a holiday atmosphere.

As for me, tension simmered and I was running on adrenaline.

And, apart from the salty water, there was another snake in the woodpile. Sixteen-year-old Ilyas, my constant companion in Zaria, was seriously getting on my nerves. Always lively, bright, sharp and funny, he had lapsed into some kind of atavistic role-play as soon as he laid eyes on Yassine and the striking older A'isha who lived with her. A'isha was very beautiful with her strong classical features – though I was startled the first time I glimpsed her stretched breasts, astonished at the combination of worn body and lovely face. Her children were with their father's family in Agadez – she was divorced.

So Ilyas, who cheerfully cooked and shopped for me, was suddenly languishing in a state of helplessness with the women waiting on his every move – not because he was a man but because he was a guest. To irritate me further he had taken to wearing a red hat with white polka-dots that he had picked up in the market in Agadez. This annoyed the life out of me because I knew he was getting into all my photo-frames and spoiling them with the jarring effect of his hat. Apart from which, normally it was a pleasure for me to look at him – he graced my days with shoulder-length blue-black hair, almond eyes alive with intelligence, a dazzling smile and light graceful hand-movements with a certain feminine air. Now all I saw was red polka-dot.

And worse again – or better from his point of view – he had bashed his head severely against the roof of the Land Cruiser when I drove too confidently into a rut, as Jimmy Cliff tried to find his way across those rivers, and had a bruise and a little cut to show for it. The headaches which resulted had to be treated by firm applications of the women's hands as he lay with his teenage head in curving laps swathed in soft black cotton.

I was not at all surprised to return from the market one day to find that my Haruna had developed a splitting headache and was likewise reclining, in A'isha's lap. Mind you, her comfort was not too earnest. "*Kai!* Get up! Bastard!" she cried laughingly in Tamajegh, cuffing his head. "Worthless Akli!" An Akli – one of the black Tuareg slave caste, the Iklan.

Haruna knew enough Tamajegh to understand but this didn't shift him or the blissful smile from his toothy face. "I not Akli!" he answered in his brave brand of broken Tamajegh. "I Nigerian. You – you worthless bushwoman!"

"*Kai!* You're a black person!" She frowned fiercely in mock anger, pointing a taut finger at his face. "Before the French came we could sell you at the market in Agadez!"

The insult rolled off Haruna like water off a duck's back. He, a Nigerian, a citizen of Africa's leading nation, was too confident of his place in life, too conscious of his superiority to any bunch of destitute bushmen to be much bothered. A natural comic, he gave as good as he got and was always the centre of attention. They loved fun and he gave it to them in bucketfuls.

But I always suffered at the slave taunts. Anger flared up like a kerosene stove out of control. And I had to stamp on it.

I wondered whether I was held in much more esteem than Haruna – I was the *Takafart*, the female Infidel, and they referred to me like that all the time. Every time I heard it, it pained me, underlining as it did my inescapable and ineradicable difference. Besides, they were notoriously lax Muslims themselves . . .

*What do I care for mallams or prayers?*
*Give me a fine camel and the beautiful Maryama . . .*

On the second day there we were in the mud hut, sweating it out through the angry midday heat, when A'isha came in and whispered something to Yassine. She then opened a scrap of knotted cloth. I thought at first it was tobacco inside but then saw it was a green powdered herb of some sort. Then I thought it was henna – and perhaps it was. Whispering conspiratorially, A'isha shuffled it into the palm of her hand with the African care not to lose a grain or a drop of any food or sustenance and held it up beneath Yassine's nipple. Then, to my astonishment, she began to squeeze Yassine's plump breast with her other hand. A thin drop dribbled out and they exclaimed together in annoyance and tried again. A few drops again. A'isha shook her head and then took the blue-brown indigoed nipple firmly between first and second finger and began to milk it more vigorously. The milk began to spurt out onto the little mound of herbs in A'isha's hand. An exclamation of satisfaction from both of them – while I felt my face flame in embarrassment and consternation – and she milked the breast again. The thin bluish milk spurted. Then A'isha mixed the herb into a paste with a little finger and with a pleased murmur carried it outside. I leant at an angle so that I could see her and there she was, kneeling next to Ilyas where he lay on a mat in the shade of the palm-trees, parting his hair to apply her poultice to the wound on his head. I thought I might faint with the tumult of feelings that rushed through me and I couldn't even define what they were. Jealousy was certainly one of them. I knew I was both revolted and furiously envious of their easy acceptance of the animal self. It raised my hackles.

And what right had Yassine – she, the grieving widow I had dragged myself a thousand kilometres to find – what right had she to be so cheerfully supplying breast milk for a malingering teenager?

I knew this patchwork of jealousy and revulsion and fascination was deeply suspect. Reduced to its simplest terms, I didn't like to find my antibiotic cream being supplanted by another woman's breast-milk – something beyond my powers to supply. But it wasn't simple.

Yassine was saying something to me about camel's milk being better if they had been able to get any. I smiled as best I could.

Ilyas looked in my direction and caught me glowering around the corner of the doorway. He grinned weakly, acting up the part of wounded hero. Then his expression shifted, a delicate frown appearing between his brows. "What's the matter with you?" he called, ever quick and sensitive to my changes of mood – except in the case of the polka-dot hat.

"Nothing," I grunted.

He shrugged gracefully. A few minutes later he maddened me further by pulling on the bloody polka-dots over his poultice.

That evening, lying by the pool, I couldn't get the image of the herbal poultice and Yassine's co-operative nipple out of my mind. The intimacy and sensuality of the act still overwhelmed me, until I was heartsick.

I wanted Amodi. I wanted the warmth of his body and the smoothness of his muscles and the rhythm of his breathing and the flash of his zany grin and the curve of his buttocks under thin cotton and the sound of his chuckle and the silky feel of his long braids as they swung against my face when he fucked me.

I wanted to be not alone, wanted to be one with him.

I turned away from the group, laid my head on a leather pillow and pretended to sleep. Then the clear distant sounds and the soft warm caress of lazy conversation around me soothed me and I did sleep.

# Chapter 5

"Ellen," said Haruna indicating Muhane with a movement of his head, "I'm going to wash that girl."

And wash her he did, with the proficiency of one who has watched children being washed thoroughly and economically from a single bucket or calabash of water every day of his childhood on the green moist plateau of Jos in Nigeria.

The result was spectacular. Her skin changed from dusty

beige to gold, her stiff scraggy halo of dusty hair sprang into
gleaming black curls and a truly gorgeous little girl emerged
enthusiastically surveying herself in my handmirror. Haruna
and I went to the market and bought her a pair of blue
rubber sandals, a small green and gold striped top and a bit
of plain royal blue cotton for a wrapper. She was
unrecognisable. I pondered on how odd it was that Yassine
should make no attempt to wash her. But that was the way
of the desert – children ran naked and wild – often in the
bitter cold, adorned only with a few blue beads and a few
leather-encased charms, until some mysterious alarm-bell
sounded – puberty, I suppose – and suddenly they were
kitted out in clothes and headdresses and sandals and
jewellery, with braided hair and oiled skin. Was it economy
or what? Or a superstition? The Evil Eye, maybe, would be
attracted if any attention was lavished on them. Who
knows, we might be blamed yet if any accident or disease
befell Muhane.

Tiny little Raechitu, in her beads and charms and blue
dye, we left as she was. By the third day she was playing with
an opened condensed milk can. The orange and white
beach ball had disappeared. I didn't ask.

Staying in In-Gall was proving expensive. Troops of men
came by all the time, either to survey us or visit the women.
They sprawled all over the place, spindly legs propped on
bony knees, and had to be given tea and fed. Haruna was
constantly being sent to the market (on my money) and
given instructions about cooking. We needed to leave before
the money gave out altogether but I had to wait for the
natural moment – too soon would be offensive.

Courtship was, in fact, rampant though muted, with the men also having a go at me. I didn't know how to square it all off with the fact that Yassine was just newly widowed but, after all, it would soon be a priority for her to find a new provider. In truth, I still hadn't perceived anything that could be called grief but, then again, there could be any amount of pain hidden beneath that mask of serenity. And living hand to mouth, fearing for the very survival of one's children, would take the edge off any grief. But I wondered why she was not living with her kinfolk or Yusuf's parents and what the alliance between her and A'isha was all about.

A'isha begged from me constantly and I ended up giving her two of the few wrappers I had with me. She, in return, sent Ilyas to the market – on my money – to buy plastic coloured thread from which she wove a bunch of intricately patterned bracelets in the inevitable blue and black with touches of white and red and green. I sat and watched her nimble supple fingers, fascinated at her skill.

"You must come back for the *Cure Salée* – the Salt Cure," she begged, halting in her weaving, her face alive with excitement. "Every year all the Tamajegh people gather, with the Arabs and the Wodaabe and others – from all over Niger! Many, many, many people! They bring their animals to lick salt and it is a time of great festivity with drumming and singing and dancing and courtship. You must come!"

In-Gall was obviously an ideal place for an unattached Tuareg woman to be – I had been intrigued to notice that even now the unmarried A'isha didn't always sleep alone.

"But come at any time – we are always here," she

69

whispered urgently. "Always in In-Gall. Any time you come back, you will find us here. Any time."

"But what if you marry again?" I asked. "A man from the desert?"

"No, no," she said vehemently. "If you come, you will find us here. In In-Gall."

Was she hunting for a husband from among the townsmen? I took the plunge. "Are you trying to marry a rich man, A'isha?" I said jokingly. "Maybe a merchant, a Hausa *Alhaji* who has been to Mecca?"

"Never, never!" she cried, shaking a finger vigorously. "The Hausa men marry four wives! Our men marry only one! I could never live with another woman! I could not have patience with that!"

And I was reminded of the extraordinary fact that Tuareg men, though entitled as Muslims to the prescribed four wives, generally shun polygamy, favouring a brand of monogamy which is emphatically serial but monogamy nevertheless.

A thought struck me. "Did you want to leave your last husband, A'isha? Or was it he who wanted to divorce you?"

"*Kai!* I left him." She said no more, busying herself again with her bracelet-making.

I didn't doubt her. Very often it was the women who walked out – literally – on a marriage, another indication of the high status of the women in this traditionally matriarchal society. Traditionally, inheritance and succession were passed through the mother's side giving women a power and respect rare in African society and unique in the Muslim world. When the French first came they took the Tuareg women to be promiscuous as mythical

South Sea Islanders, so free and independent were their manners.

I was losing count of the days we had stayed, uneasily aware that we were settling in as if it were home. A little daily routine was being established. Every morning dawned with a bit of brigandage – Haruna and Ilyas had taken to grabbing passing goats and pulling them into our hut where, with Haruna holding them by the head, Ilyas milked them into a big purple plastic cup. We drank the warm, sweet, foaming milk feeling very clever and guilty. Then visitors began to arrive and we generally held court throughout the day, falling asleep on our mats in the sweltering heat of midday, waking to drag the mats outside and wait for sunset, the coolness of evening and the stars. Sometimes we went to the market in the mornings or to spend the day in other households. In the late afternoons I took to wandering around with the children in the cool of the gardens under the shade of the date palms; we bought the huge tomatoes and melons grown there and ate them as we walked.

Ataka, of course, was plying his trade, producing rings and necklaces for anyone who could come up with a piece of silver or gold.

And A'isha was constantly begging me to forget Tazerza and stay in In-Gall.

While all this was going on, I felt like a diver poised on a high-board.

We had to move on.

We were loading up the obligatory gifts of sacks of millet in the market, getting ready to leave, when I saw the old man,

Yusuf's father, approaching on a donkey at a trot. He was dressed in cheap white cotton, rather than the formal black or indigo. Above the white veil of his *tagilmoust*, his eyes were wary.

We confronted each other – snake-catcher and snake – which was which? He asked to speak to me privately.

In the gloom of a nearby tin-roofed shack, he gently reprimanded me in a mixture of clumsy Hausa, Tamajegh and sign language, for giving his son's money to Yassine. She was a beautiful young woman, she would marry again quickly, she was no good and didn't care about him and his wife. She had already refused to live with them even before Yusuf had died. But where were he and Yusuf's mother to find money to live? Yusuf used to take care of them – they had no other son – what would happen to them now?

I cursed myself for getting it so wrong – he was right, of course – Yassine had resources, he had not. Then I did the only thing I could – I lied and said I would speak to Yusuf's *maigida* and would return to In-Gall as soon as I could and I would bring some money for them. I suppose I meant it at the time. But in fact I never went back to In-Gall.

We were practically on our way when I saw the small procession approaching: Yassine, the children and some boys bearing a trunk, a mat, a *bidon* for water. A'isha brought up the rear with a face like thunder. Yassine and the children were coming with us to Tazerza, to visit her sister who lived in neighbouring Tassara.

I tried to talk her out of it, as did A'isha vehemently. We wouldn't be coming back through In-Gall so she might be stranded. But she was adamant – she was coming with us.

So then we had to add another two sacks of grain to the

roof-rack – for the sister. Jesus. We'd be lucky if we didn't snap an axle with this load – eight sacks of grain and the extra passengers with their gear, besides me, Haruna, Ilyas, Ataka and ours.

So we set out, heading along the sandy road to the north-east at first, as if we were returning to Agadez. Then we circled north, cutting across the track which led to Teguidda-n-Tessoumt, and headed west, speeding along the harsh dry flatlands. To the south was Tchin Tabaraden and ahead of us Tazerza with its goatskin tents in their dry-season resting-places. There, an arm's-length away, was Amodi. I had my joy in my sights now and it could not escape me.

At night we slept on mats on the level sand and one night, as we lay beneath a glaring stupendous moon, a party of Tuareg appeared like apparitions risen out of the sand, speaking in quiet murmurs. Women emerged from the group and insisted on rigging up a bed for me with carved wooden posts they took from the back of their camels. Tightly woven leather and straw mats were laid on top and dyed leather pillows.

They had come east from the Azaouagh area and had passed through the dry-season camp of Ilyas's people. Was Sideka there? Yes. Had they been anywhere near Amodi's encampment? No – but yes, they had news of him – yes, he was well. Yes, he was there.

# Chapter 6

*Tazerza, Niger*

But Amodi was not there when we arrived. My pride forbade me even to ask about him so I spent the first morning in an agony of suspense, sitting at the door of a goatskin tent smiling at the world – furious with Haruna and Ilyas that they didn't have the wits to ask about him and tell me where he was – thinking at any moment to have a

74

sudden sight of him striding eagerly over the sand. I was also afraid to ask – afraid of what I might hear.

Eventually his mother, Tsalert, a fine-boned tiny elderly-looking woman with a lovely face, casually remarked that he was at a household "away to the north" but "he was coming". I pretended indifference while feverishly wondering: how far, how long? But what was the point in asking? They only understood distances in terms of time and time in the desert was an ever-flexible and fluid commodity. They would despise signs of impatience – think it comic and ridiculous.

I smiled at Tsalert, praying that she would tell me more but she did not.

I loved Tsalert. Because of him. And wanted her to love me. But she never really acknowledged any special relationship between us, despite the fact that I always showered her with presents – thick rolls of soft black cloth, strings of beads, Maria Theresa silver coins to have jewellery made and, of course, the all-important sacks of grain. She needed all the support I could give her. She had been divorced from Amodi's father many years before, and had gone away to Tassara in the north leaving the ten-year-old Amodi behind. Since then she had married several times but there had been no other surviving children. When her last husband died, leaving her destitute, Amodi, her only child, had gone and brought her back to Tazerza. It was an unhappy situation – Amodi's father was dead and Tsalert had to live side by side with Maryam his widow.

Amodi felt fiercely protective of her and I would have done the world and all for her if she had responded to me a bit more. But she remained slightly aloof. Perhaps it was the universal policy of "if I pretend it isn't there maybe it will go away". My own mother back in Ireland stuck to much the same policy.

They slaughtered two goats on our arrival. I always felt half-guilty, knowing how precious each animal was now after the droughts. But it was a matter of pride for them – hospitality being a great virtue. It was strange – whenever I tried to come up with a word to describe that trait of theirs I could only come up with the Irish word *fláithiúlacht*, which means the virtue of being hospitable and open-handed, a concept springing from our own feudal system. We still use the word in Ireland as if there were no English equivalent that expresses the notion and there are other words – *grámhar*, for instance, which means loving, warm, demonstrative in the same larger-than-life sense.

The Tuareg have a special word for "hunger for meat" and my arrival gave them the opportunity to satisfy that, living on a spartan diet of millet with milk as they did.

I watched the hapless goats being held, neck to the ground, the clean slit across the throat executed with an accompanying prayer – and indeed they would starve rather than eat an animal which was slaughtered without the requisite prayer – the brief jerking of the body as the eyes glazed over, life departing visibly, spilling like the blood in the sand. And as always it amazed me how quick and clean it was. As indeed was the rest of the process. I had always imagined skinning would be like a gory scalping in Hollywood westerns but, instead, the skin was stripped from the hanging carcass in a clean and bloodless way – for all the world like a jumpsuit being unzipped and stripped off, leaving the naked body.

We ate the tender meat shredded and oiled and seasoned in a large wooden bowl, passing the wooden spoon from one person to the other.

Three days passed with no sign or news of Amodi. I hung between painful tension and the joy of knowing that, if I had to sit on my mat for a month, sooner or later I would be in his physical presence. Zaria was just a wraith-like presence at the back of my mind, unreal as a mirage. I sat on my mat and waited and watched.

The women sat there, dark eyes glinting, draped in indigo-steeped soft black cotton, their babies suckling at firm brown breasts. Placid, good-humoured, they chewed tobacco, drank sweet tea and chased for lice in each other's glossy blue-black hair. As always, I was repelled by the animality of it all. Fascinated with it. Envied them that.

"Ellen!" they cried. "Stay here with us and drink camel's milk until you become a beautiful woman! *Big!*" They made circles with their arms to show how big. They spoke to me in clumsy Hausa and often made remarks in Tamajegh which they assumed I didn't understand, unaware that I knew enough to follow conversations.

They rubbed indigo dye into the insides of my arms, marvelling at how luminous it looked on my pale skin. "Beautiful!" they said. I was pleased that at least in one small way they granted that I surpassed them – I could make indigo glow better.

One laughing young woman, Djanetta, was particularly energetic in courting my friendship. She hadn't been in the camp when I visited before. Djanetta fell more than a little short of the Tuareg ideal of beauty – her teeth were large and her lips too generous so her constant expression was a huge toothy grin in a face full of lively warmth. Her voice was shrill and nasal. She struck me, oddly, as the type who might be a nun back home. Like Yassine, she was a tiny woman – it seemed as if Tuareg girls were genetically programmed to grow outwards instead of upwards in their teens, while the boys strode on to become tall and sinewy.

Little as Djanetta was, her breasts and buttocks stuck out aggressively. In the desert, I mused, a childbearer had to have the capacity to store fat – like a camel – the buttocks being the hump.

Yet the desert was full of contradictions that constantly confounded me. The women of the neighbouring tribe, the Peuhl, stalked stork-like through the landscape with graceful elongated frames, bearing their enormous calabashes of milk on their heads. Aquiline faces delicately tattooed, hair gathered into a huge top-knot on the forehead, each ear pierced a dozen times around the edge with huge hoops of some light metal like tin, wearing short little bodices which left the lower half of their breasts bare and short skirts of woven striped cloth – they were fantastic figures against a surreal landscape, like something out of the post-nuclear world of *Mad Max*. And lean, very lean.

I could but marvel at this miracle of ethnic survival, these two separate cultures living side by side over the centuries, never intermingling. And, for me, there was a flip-side even to this miracle – the thought that it was yet another symptom of a self-absorption I found threatening.

Djanetta smeared blue dye liberally on me at every

opportunity. "Beautiful!" she cried, slapping one supple finger on her palm and flicking it through a loose fist. And she pulled two dark-blue bracelets from her arms and put them on mine. Crude circles of glass, they glowed marvellously in the sun.

The old men fretted at the way my hair hung about my face "like a madwoman". Finally, when Abu Bakr, Amodi's uncle and head of the extended family group, began to fuss about my hair I agreed to go through the lengthy process of plaiting. So Zainabu, Amodi's little half-sister, padded off to get some hair-gel from another tent. A year before she would have scampered like a young gazelle but now she was about twelve and at that age they would be getting her to eat up and become fat and beautiful. She was very beautiful, very like Amodi, with full lips, almond-shaped eyes, delicate brows and a perfect luminous oval face.

Lying on my side, supported by a leather pillow under my armpit, I tried to make the best of an embarrassing situation. I'd had this experience inflicted on me before and I hadn't liked it then either.

Yassine, still with us, was elected to do my hair. She smathered a copious amount of the blue hair-gel they used onto her palms and began to smear it vigorously on my hair. I hated the gooey gel for starters and then there was the effort of concealing the fact that I didn't have the suppleness or muscular tone to keep poised in that position for a long period of time without strain. Nor did it help that I knew enough of the language to understand when Zainabu's mother, Maryam (a handsome heavy-boned woman not at all like her little sylph of a daughter) muttered "Ears on her head!" – meaning that my ears stuck out at more than the accepted angle.

They tut-tutted over the red-brown colour of my hair.

"El-len!" Maryam cried in her drawling tone. They always cried my name out shrilly as if I were deaf. "There is a trader who comes sometimes – a Hausaman – and he has a hair-dye – black-black – if he comes we will buy some for you! It will make your hair very very black – beautiful!"

I raised a feeble grin. Fuck their black hair. It irritated the hell out of me that they could see no beauty or merit in anything that was strange or different.

Yassine was working away busily, various little blunt knives used to twist sections of my hair into knots and pin them out of the way. She flashed a scrap of broken mirror before me a few times and I saw that, as ever, she had chosen a style where an intricate structure of tiny plaits projected low onto my forehead and ran down the sides of my face. I thought it made me look like a pig – but of course they loved that chubby look.

"Good!" smiled Abu Bakr when the process was at last finished, running his gnarled hands with pleasure over the intricate result. I was uncomfortable and self-conscious – it felt tight about my head and, sure enough, it made my ears stick out more than usual. I smiled.

I tied my dark-blue headscarf around it, covering it up, and felt better.

It was all absorbing and wonderful but it was difficult. If I had been with Amodi, soul and body singing with the joy of his presence, it would have been so much easier. But I was heartsore, anxiety and longing and impatience eating away at me. It was hard to be gracious, it was hard to be fun, to give all passers-by their money's worth entertainment-wise.

When I felt like lying down and dying with the nervous strain of waiting and wondering.

And of course there was sweet damn all privacy. I was on show at all times, to all people. The kids formed a constant border of grinning faces to my every activity. And if I just sat, they sat and stared. I was used to this exposure to an extent even in Zaria, where I constantly wore dark glasses to the market or wherever, so I didn't have to make eye-contact with all the staring eyes. And where, even in my own house, I literally had to lock myself up in my bedroom to get a moment alone – and then they'd be knocking at the door, knocking at the window – they just had no concept of private space. The local Nigerians were better – they had some concepts of privacy – from the colonial experience of working as servants but primarily from their own culture where, for instance, rich *Alhajis* kept their wives in a form of liberal purdah. It was the difference between living in mud architecture and living in leather tents.

What I needed was a great black veil like the Tuareg women – turn the back, pull the veil down over the face and spread it wide and that signalled a claiming of space, a little nodule of privacy around the woman. But I didn't have a veil, they couldn't interpret my subtle signals and I didn't know theirs, and they stared without mercy.

# Chapter 7

On the third day, when he hadn't come, I did stir from my mat. Ilyas was fretful and eager to see his home and I had to find Sideka. Their household was a couple of hours to the west, I was told. A couple of hours? By foot? By camel? Yes, by camel, of course. How long in a car? They didn't know.

Ataka was busy. He would stay and wait for us. He had set up his little anvil and was plying his trade, with no apparent inclination to go off and find the family he had been pining for while he was in Zaria. All in good time, I supposed. There was, after all, all the time in the world, wasn't there? And he was in business.

We set off in the morning in the Land Cruiser, scanning the landscape for animal or human form. Haruna was driving, his buck-toothed face alive under a faint grey coating of dust. In his native Jos, on the plateau, his jet-black skin would gleam with washing and oil.

We had the elderly Abu Bakr as navigator.

"Bushman, for fuck's sake!" said Haruna in English, pointing with his lips at Abu Bakr who was squeezed next to me and Ilyas in the passenger seat.

I soon saw what he meant. Abu Bakr was incapable of giving directions without leaning out of the car. If he wanted to indicate "right", he leant out precariously through the left-hand window and pointed around the edge of the windscreen.

What he was recognising in that monotonous landscape I could not say but by mid-morning we came in sight of a group of tents in the far distance, sheltered in a bunch of dried thorn bushes and a couple of acacia trees.

The old man gestured vigorously.

Ilyas started to argue with him, a long forefinger waving back and forth in an emphatic negative. "No, no, not at all!" He knew his own home-tents even at that distance. "Pass them, Haruna! They should be somewhere here but that's not them. Go round them lest they delay us."

The camp had exploded into activity at the sight and sound of the Land Cruiser but the running figures had fallen back disappointed when they saw us circle to the left.

We were leaving the tents behind and had passed a bunch of naked kids who stood open-mouthed, staring at us, before it even registered.

"*Go back! Go back!*" I cried.

"What?" Haruna glowered at me.

"Go back! I've just seen something!"

We circled back to the children.

"Look!"

The sand was dotted with little black pieces of cloth. I leapt out with the camera. It was a toy encampment. Why I should have been so surprised at this most natural of phenomena, I don't know. They were playing doll's houses, each little tent a piece of black cloth carefully erected on sticks no more than six inches high, each complete and perfect with mats and beds inside – and even a tiny swinging wicker cradle, painstakingly woven, with a bundle in it! Outside were fires and cooking pots. Clay camels stood at the tent doors and small creatures stood around – goats or dogs, I couldn't tell.

Best of all – on each mat sat a little woman draped in black or indigo blue.

Ilyas reached into a tent and lifted out a figure to show me, unwrapping the cloth veil.

"Oh, God! It's the Venus of the Sahara!" And there she sat, as she had from prehistoric times: a woman, but a woman sitting as she would inside a tent. The head hardly existed but the hair which was twisted into a topknot was carefully modelled. No face. The breasts stuck out aggressively, pointed. The main features were the swelling belly and the great jutting curves of the hips. No legs – where did she have to go, this queen bee, sitting there wallowing in her fertility? Why should she need a face? The fat on her buttocks was much more useful. Venus de Milo might have lost an arm or two – she's had a few hard knocks over the centuries after all – but this Venus was never intended to have limbs. This was the quintessential female honey-pot made clay.

We put the little figure, this little household goddess, back in her appointed place and I got my camera and took several dozen photos of the children and their work of art while Ilyas and our navigator established that Sideka's encampment was not far ahead of us.

We reached it only ten minutes later.

A few dogs ran to meet us, barking, and in their wake a flurry of people – half-cautious, half-eager – hesitating, rushing – children of all sizes running towards us and then away like little naked gazelles. Abu Bakr, true to form, hoarsely shouted names and greetings oblivious to the fact that nothing could be heard at that distance over the roar of the engine. Then Ilyas hauled him firmly in by his shirt and, perched on the window frame, hung out precariously, joyfully waving.

We alighted into a cluster of madly excited people and Ilyas's mother came running, dusty black wrapper trailing as she stumbled half-fainting in her fright and joy. I cried to see it and cried to see her clasp him and the awfulness of what I was here to do began to flutter at my heart.

And yet I was resolved to do it.

Sideka was not in the crowd. We drank water and fizzy sharp fermented milk and then, out of politeness, had to laugh and joke through the tea ceremony and give the news.

But in this case I had Ilyas's eagerness working on my side and soon we went to look for Sideka.

We wound our way through thorn bushes in the Land Cruiser: me, Haruna, Ilyas, a clutch of naked wild-haired children and two clothed grinning teenagers who perched and swayed, muscles tensed, hands gripping the car-seats as if they were riding camels.

They were pointing something out to me well before I could see anything in the hazy distance. Soon they were plucking at my shirt, repeating with conviction "Sideka – Sideka!" while I could still see little more than a dancing mirage puppet figure.

I strained my eyes and was no surer as we drew nearer. And then, at last, something in the movement or perhaps just an instinct told me it was him. And with that instinct came the urgent thought that it might be better to stop and get out rather than bearing down on him out of the blue. He would recognise the car – had done so already without a doubt but nevertheless I felt he should have the time to adjust to the sight of his inescapable destiny bearing down on him in the shape of a bright blue Land Cruiser and an array of multicoloured grinning faces.

Would he expect to see Mike among the faces, I wondered?

I got Haruna to halt. We clambered out and walked to meet the lithe figure which was approaching us steadily but without haste.

It was Sideka, suddenly close enough for me to see the solemnity of his expression. He was wearing sky-blue traditional trousers and a scrap of a white cotton shirt. I wondered if he still had all the clothes he had brought from Zaria – given everything away, no doubt.

He came loping out of the shimmer of midday, a gangly

fifteen-year-old with the beautiful severe face of a Tutankhamun in tranquillity – a face which I knew could split into an ironic dazzling wry grin in a flash. There was some of that wryness now on that face. But I would never manage to gauge what he felt on seeing us. Too young to wear a *tagilmoust*, he was nevertheless assuming the rigid dignity and gravity the Tuareg always assume on greeting friends or foes. I marvelled at such poise, such control.

But my Haruna, striding on ahead, put paid to his dignity in no time. With a whoop and an explosion of abuse in three languages – *"Goats, for God's sake! A fucking goatboy!"* – he grappled with Sideka and they were locked in a wrestling-hold, hysterical with laughter, by the time we reached them.

That was one of my first memories of him – locked in a head-hold with my Haruna – and I had looked at him and thought *"That one"*.

We had found Sideka on one of our trips to Katsina, just south of the Nigerien border. He was one of a swarm of kids living with their families on a building site – there were more women and children in Katsina, being close to the border, than one normally found further south. We had gone to record a certain Tuareg singer, a man with a voice of echoing, soaring hair-raising resonance. We had stayed late, listening to the men make the night throb with rhythms driven by urgent hand-clapping, voices vibrant with a barely reined excitement. And always, in the rich echoing throat-deep cries was a cold keen edge that reflected the glitter of the remote stars. I couldn't tear myself away and we decided to stay until the next day.

Sideka had sung that night with a confidence and

strength that amazed me, his brother Ilyas providing the backing responses. A thought had been straying through my head – I wanted a boy who could teach me Tamajegh, as Haruna was teaching me Hausa. But strangely, it wasn't until the following day, when I saw him doubled up in hysterical play with Haruna, that I thought "That one". It was his vitality that attracted me.

We took him back to Zaria with us, with his parents' permission. Ilyas soon followed us and found work on one of the building sites on the university campus, while the rest of the family retreated north. Perhaps there was some notion that, with two sons bearing the burden of bringing home the booty and one actually living under the patronage of an affluent foreign woman, they could safely retire to Niger.

Sideka lived in my house for a month only. My friend Mike came by frequently, as usual. The boys also went and visited him and always came back with giggling, mocking but affectionate tales of Mike's eccentricities. Mike, of course, spoke Hausa rather well which earned him a certain respect from the lads. He was a settled resident of Zaria in a way few expatriates were and had previously lived in the old walled city where there were few foreigners.

Then one day he paid me a formal and very nervous visit. Asking my permission to take Sideka to live with him. He would employ him, pay him to help in the house and garden and he would send him to school. The boy was strikingly bright and deserved such a chance. Apparently Sideka had already agreed. I don't remember being hurt at Sideka's defection. Must have been. Must have wondered why. Must have wondered if it was just the money. But I can't remember any of that.

So Mike asked me and I said yes.

I cannot say to this day why I said yes.

We drove back to camp, the lads setting the tone for the kind of giddy high we often experienced when together.

"God Almighty, this bastard of a goatboy has brought us into the bush," shouted Haruna, buck-teeth gleaming in joy. "Fuck him! He's brought us trouble! Better we hang the bastard on that bit of a thing they call a tree in this bastard country!"

"So what brought *you* here?" Ilyas asked.

"This European woman's madness brought me here! Ah, Nigeria! Nigeria! Why did I leave my Nigeria?" yelled Haruna, a grin of delight pasted across his face.

"*Akli!* Worthless slave!" shouted Sideka in equal glee, chuckling in that distinctive slightly hoarse voice of his. "You with your teeth like an elephant! We'll sell you and you'll be taken to Algeria! You'll never see your Nigeria again! Wait until we get back to the camp – we'll give you a pestle and put you pounding grain!"

"Fuck your pestle!" Haruna was, as usual, impervious to insult. "Wait until we get back! Until I put a pestle up your ass!"

Music to my ears.

Late that afternoon I asked Sideka to step aside with me for a talk – or, rather, I got up from my mat and made the lip and eye movements that said "Follow me". This was the approved method of requesting a confidential chat in an environment which didn't have rooms or houses or sheds or bars or loos or gardens or cars or churches or motels – only the next sand-dune.

We walked a small distance from the camp – further than your regular word-in-your-ear type exchange merited – and sat down on fine white sand, facing each other. He was wearing a flowing white cotton robe over the small cotton shirt. His eyes were heavily outlined in kohl.

I noted the gravity of his expression with misgiving.

He began to play with the sand, sifting it through his fingers.

We sat, a boy and a woman, neither of us wearing the *tagilmoust*, both of us wearing masks.

I began to speak, formally, in English. "Well, Sideka, how is it that you didn't come back – " I stopped in embarrassment at the stilted coldness of my voice, flat and false to my ears. Why had I always to pretend I didn't care? Shouldn't I shout at him? Speak with passion, at least? No, I couldn't. Chameleon-like, I had to fade into the background and be stoical, as they were. I'd lived with them too long.

Besides, I was afraid of what he might say. Most of all I was afraid he might tell me the truth. Tell me he wouldn't come back with me. Tell me why.

"Well . . ." He hesitated. A twist of the mouth. "*Kai*, I'm coming back," he muttered, eyes downcast.

Relief swept through my body: it was OK, he was going to lie.

I lapsed back into Hausa, now more confident. "Your *maigida* is very worried because you haven't returned to school, *surtout* because you were going ahead with it so well."

"Yes . . . I know." He still hadn't looked at me.

"You know that you are very very late? That you are many weeks behind. You didn't tell the truth when you said you would be back without a doubt."

"I know. But . . . my father was sick . . . he needed someone to mind the goats . . . "

"Had he no one at all to help him? What of his Iklan?"

"All our slaves are gone to Nigeria . . . "

"Your father asked you to stay?"

"Yes."

"But you wanted to go back?"

"Yes, I wanted to." He raised his eyes and looked at me. *"Very much,"* he said emphatically.

I neither believed nor disbelieved him. This was pseudo-communication. There was nothing honest being said by either of us. What was the point?

The point was, as ever, to go through the conventional motions and see how things fell out at the final throw of the dice.

I wondered suddenly if there was a girl. Probably, with the Tuareg passion for courtship. I must ask Ilyas and Haruna.

Jesus, when all was said and done, he was probably just enjoying himself around here, having a great old time, being the returned traveller. Probably had every intention of going back to Zaria . . . but tomorrow . . .

And Amodi?

A sudden war-whoop split the air. Ilyas and Haruna were striding over the sand. Great. Same problem as always. If I were a Tuareg woman they wouldn't dream of bouncing in on a *tête à tête*. With an eccentric Infidel woman, normal rules need not apply.

"*To*," I said to Sideka. "I'll talk to your father."

"Ellen!" Now Ilyas was within hailing distance. "El-len!"

I waved. He started to make the hand movement that used to baffle me so much when I first came to Africa. Hand outstretched, palm down, fingers snapping inward to the palm – it still looked like "go" rather than "come" to me, even now when I used it myself.

I got up and headed towards them as they veered off to the left. Sideka stayed sitting, still fiddling with the sand.

Ilyas had something to show me.

We arrived at a solitary tent standing alone, with some small acacia trees around it. We squatted down outside – or they squatted, I sat – and Ilyas went through the greetings. A woman's voice answered from the recesses of the tent but no one appeared. Ilyas fell silent, hand to head, seeming a little perplexed. I was staring, fascinated, at one of the trees which was festooned with a mixed collection of belongings – rolled mats, sides of meat, cooking pots, sandals, wire braziers.

A desultory bit of conversation started up with long pauses between responses. I couldn't follow it very well. Then we waited silently – but there was no movement.

I looked questioningly at Ilyas and he indicated with his lips towards a cluster of items hanging from a tent-pole – the slim wooden writing tablets *mallams* used, some crammed with painstakingly written Arabic, bottles of ink bound in leather and a leather-bound thick tome which must have been a handwritten *Koran*.

Eventually Ilyas shrugged, rose to his feet and moved off. We followed.

"Who was that?" I asked when we were out of earshot.

"A woman *mallam*," he said. "Her name is Fatima."

I was astounded. I had never heard of such a thing. A *woman*? A woman *mallam* – a religious teacher?

"She lives by herself. But she refused to greet you. She said she couldn't greet a *Takafart*."

*Takafart*. Infidel. It was ironic. A remarkable woman in such a role. And she couldn't talk to me because I was an Infidel.

But I was too knocked out by the fact of her existence to be outraged about that. What an amazing people! An Islamic society that allowed a woman teacher? What was she? A hermit? I thought of the little Venus of the Sahara, the little fertility goddess, all breasts and belly and buttocks, no limbs, no head. And here was another side to the coin – a woman with hands to write and eyes to read and a brain to think and teach. And the power of *choice*. To choose to live the life of a hermit. It was stunning.

I looked at Ilyas's laughing face with renewed respect. What a marvellous fucking heritage.

Aghali, Sideka's father, was a most unimpressive little man. I always met him with a renewed sense of astonishment that he had produced my wonderful Ilyas to say nothing of the remarkable Sideka. But, leaving the physical beauty aside, where was the wit and the intelligence that darted from his sons like wildfire?

A fact that troubled me was that Sideka looked set to grow head and shoulders above his father and older brother just by virtue of the fact he ate vegetables and meat every day in Mike's house. As indeed my Haruna looked set to tower over the stocky muscular members of his family. It was a frightening and uneasy fact to live with. Now, when it was maybe too late, Ilyas was doing a lot of his eating in my house.

I was lucky to find Aghali alone when I went there just before sundown. Abu Bakr had gone off with the lads in the Land Cruiser to visit a neighbouring camp and Sideka's mother was out of the way. Apparently, as soon as she laid hands on the few gifts and money Ilyas had brought for her, she had high-tailed it off on a donkey to the nearest Inaden camp to trade her goods for silver and gold pieces and have jewellery made.

I faced Aghali, cross-legged, across the teapot in its charcoal burner. It was our second day in his household and it was time for me to head back to Amodi's place – where surely, surely, Amodi would now be.

I was scared. I was scared he would refuse to let Sideka go, I was scared that he would tell me that Sideka didn't want to go, I was scared he would tell me *why* Sideka didn't want to go.

*Please don't tell me the truth or ask me the truth, Aghali.*

"*To*, Aghali," I said, my palms sweating. "I have a message for you from Sideka's *maigida*."

"Michael!" he said easily, with pleasure. He fiddled with his little tea-glasses, arranging them on the small brass tray. "Why did he not come with you to visit us?"

"He is working."

"Praise be to God!"

"*To*. But, you know, he is worried because Sideka has not returned to school."

He shrugged. "I am also worried."

I stared at him. Useless. None of them needed a veil to be impenetrable.

"Aghali – your son has a great head. If he stays at school, without a doubt he will be a very important person some day. Especially since he is now speaking English like an English boy, as well as French and Hausa. Not many Tuareg know English." It would indeed be a huge advantage to him.

"You know, the young have no sense. They want nothing but play. He doesn't want to work."

"So he doesn't want to go back to Zaria?"

"No, not at all!"

Using the end of his *tagilmoust* as pot-holder he plucked the little teapot from its charcoal bed and flicked back the little lid. The teapot was red enamel, decorated and mended with little patterned ovals of brass. He pushed densely textured chunks of sugar-cone inside and returned the teapot to the burner.

Tea-making was worthy of absolute attention.

The fate of his son was better left in God's hands.

I tried again. "So if he wants to go back to Zaria with me, you will let him go?"

"*Kai!* Better he go than waste his time around here!" Tea was poured into the glasses and then back into the pot to mix in the sugar. Then poured again and a glass was proffered.

I drank it off as I had learned to do, the bitterness strong enough to take the enamel off your teeth.

More water was added to the pot, more sugar. The second glass would be lighter, sweeter and the third pale gold and sweetest of all.

"You know, Ellen, our fathers made a big mistake. When the French decided that our children should go to school and came to search for them, we took our children and hid them in the bush. We gave them instead the sons of our slaves and they took them away for schooling."

"I know. And that is why you now have no powerful man in the government or the army or the police or the courts to protect your people or give them help in any way. The Djerma and the Hausa did not make that mistake."

"But we – our fathers thought we needed nothing but the desert."

He fell silent. I knew that in his heart Aghali still believed they needed nothing but the desert. If he were to allow Sideka to go back to Zaria, it would not be for the schooling. It would be for the promise of Mike's patronage – Mike, a source that would never dry up, whose money would buy back those lost herds. That was the only form of greatness and security that Aghali would ever want or understand.

"And then the droughts came . . . " He lapsed again into silence.

And as so often they did, in introspection or anxiety, and though he normally wouldn't have done it during the tea ceremony, he opened his tobacco pouch. In Nigeria it would have been a handkerchief, the tobacco knotted inside – Aghali's was a little tooled leather pouch. He pushed down the folds of his *tagilmoust* from his mouth with a practised finger and then took a pinch of tobacco from the pouch.

He paused in the act of raising it to his mouth, then lowered it again. He was not looking at me. He stared ahead at some interior landscape. Then quite softly he began to recite the words of the song Yusuf used to sing.

*"The beautiful ones are all burnt,*
*Their long hair is no longer buttered,*

*They only water American powdered milk and drink it.*
*These sisters live in misery*
*There are no oxen to trap*
*For they have, like their mothers, all vanished too.*
*But only last year, on moving camp for salt*
*At Agayya, they were all queens, young men and women*
*Sinning and making merry . . ."*

At the last word he looked at me. "Do you understand that?" he asked.

"I do. Yusuf – who died – used to sing it in Zaria."

He made a click to the back of his throat in satisfaction. The tobacco was raised and poised on his out-thrust lower lip. He chewed.

And here was the handkerchief after all, with a few nuggets of potash tied inside. A tiny piece of the bitter metallic stuff was added to the moistened wad of tobacco and chewed in.

And all this done, like the tea ceremony, with an utter concentration that made it a zen exercise even for me, the watcher.

He spat to one side, a stream of tobacco juice hitting the sand. He flicked some sand over it.

"Ellen – our people have suffered. We have seen our children starve. We survived here in this part of the country but I have heard terrible things that happened in the north. There was a man who threw all three of his children in a well and drowned them because he couldn't bear to see them starve. Their mother when she found what he had done went mad – she had one baby with her that she was breast-feeding, so she threw that one also in the well and went and hanged herself from a tree. And another man went mad and killed his children and walked the desert with their guts draped around his neck. These were not the only cases."

I didn't want to hear any of this. Couldn't bear it. Had these things really happened? Was it just their capacity for drama that came up with these stories? But it was all the one: fact or fiction, that capacity they had for violent action or violent imagining made me fearful.

"Listen!" said Aghali. He raised a finger and began to recite again:

*"I trust in Him who has goats, has Niger, has taken Diori out*
*And put in Kountche,*
*Has wiped out that one's numerous cattle*
*And left the Tuareg so destitute*
*They began to be watchmen."*

I needed to finalise something about Sideka. I was quite sure he should come with me. Things were changing. Whether they perceived it or not, there could be no return to the old opulent and powerful ways and days – the raiding and warring and slave system. There was nothing ahead but hunger and oppression and the five nations of Niger, Mali, Algeria, Burkina and Libya closing a hand that would squeeze them to death. Sideka had a chance. He must go back to Zaria.

Aghali put his wad of tobacco aside and proceeded with the tea-making. We drank the second glass and then I took from my bag the wad of naira notes that Michael had given me for him. A somewhat disparaging glance at the gift, a muttered but dignified thank you and the money was carefully tucked into the flat leather purse he wore about his neck.

They were flamboyantly generous when they could be

but they sure were lousy on the receiving side. But how could they be grateful for mean and meagre offerings from the endless supply of wealth all foreigners were believed to have?

After we drank the third glass of yellow-gold sweet-sweet tea, sharp and hot, I tried again.

"*To*, Aghali, you agree then? When I go, I will take Sideka?"

A hand made a graceful practised gesture, adjusting the folds of the *tagilmoust* over his mouth. "If he agrees, he may go."

"Doesn't he agree?"

"He doesn't want to go."

Christ.

Ask the question.

"But I don't understand that. He has a good life in Zaria. He has all he needs – food, clothes, school, money, medicine, comfort." Television, a dog, ice cream, a bicycle, a watch, a ghetto-blaster, cinema, karate lessons, swimming-pools, Coca-Cola, a bedroom of his own with mosquito-net. Blessings without end.

"You speak the truth."

Ask the question.

"So, *why* doesn't he want to go?" My heart hammered because of the answer I didn't want to hear.

"*Kai!* Young people! They have no heads!"

And he began to wash the glasses.

# Chapter 8

Four nights after we had got back I was sprawled on a mat in front of my tent, writing something by flashlight in my notebook, when all at once there was a commotion in the camp. Then I heard the Land Cruiser start up – I had left it parked at a distance when we came back from the well. Then, with the greatest of irritation, I heard it drive away. God damn! Haruna was fooling around with it without my permission – and in the dark! I scrambled to my feet and was scrabbling around for my sandals when a bunch of children came running up.

"*Radio! Radio!*" they all cried, pointing behind them.

"What has happened?" I asked.

"Spirits!" said one. "We need the radio because of the spirits!"

"What spirits? What do you mean?"

"It is Amodi's uncle!"

I was getting nowhere here. They had already dragged the radio from the tent. "*To, to,*" I said as the oldest of them hitched it up on his shoulder and they tore off in high excitement. I shoved my feet in my sandals, snapped off my torch, slung my camera round my neck and followed them.

A bunch of people came into view, standing and milling about. The radio blared out into the stillness as it scrambled full volume through the stations, then it stabilised on some traditional music and a ragged handclap started up and then swung into rhythm. I glimpsed some white object on the ground. Someone turned to me as I came up behind the group and I was startled to see familiar eyes – it took me a moment to recognise him – it was a friend from Zaria, an Akli named Kulutan, and I had never before seen him wearing a *tagilmoust*. Beyond him I saw the object, black and white, shudder and then lie quiet again. A wounded animal? Kulutan gripped my arm and drew me into the circle between him and another Akli named Chimbizat. Then I saw the object on the ground was a man.

I watched, bewildered and a bit horrified. He began to stir. Grotesquely he staggered to his feet, arms outstretched. His knees came up in turn in a high-stepping rhythmic movement. He was dancing. His *tagilmoust* had fallen loosely around his neck and the immensely long tail trailed behind him in the dust. He moved as if in slow motion inside the circle with tranced exaggerated movements, knees bent, arms stretched wide, head flung back, eyes closed. I didn't think I had seen him before but, ironically, it was difficult to recognise the men without their headdresses.

A hand gripped my elbow. Kulutan was shouting something but I couldn't hear him what with the din and the *tagilmoust* muffling his voice. I almost snatched at the *tagilmoust* in my irritation. He understood my gesture and pulled it down, putting his mouth close to my ear.

"It is Amodi's uncle!" he shouted.

"What has happened with him?" I cried.

"The spirits have entered him!"

Possession.

"He just arrived here!" shouted Chimbizat on the other side of me. "He had been travelling."

Travelling? Just arrived?

"Just now he came?" I shouted, tugging him violently by the shirt. "Did he come with Amodi?"

"Yes!"

"Yes? Where? Where is Amodi?" My eyes searched wildly in the crowd.

"He has gone with Haruna in the Landrobel to bring the drum from the next camp!" Chimbizat's white teeth flashed in a grin of pleasure above the dark folds of his *tagilmoust*.

"The drum?" My voice rose shrilly on the question.

"Yes!" shouted Kulutan. "They will sing the spirits out of him!"

The music faded and was replaced by religious discussion so they had to shut the radio off and start up a fast-paced chant, clapping in rhythm.

Then the grimacing faces were caught in the headlights of the Land Cruiser and it drew up. I saw Amodi jump out and help lift a big hemispherical drum from the back – the *ettebel*. Then I saw him and Haruna join the circle on the other side.

I felt cheated. I had waited so long and now I was reduced to just a small thing among spirits. And he – he had not thought to find me when he came. He had gone for the drum.

Now, with two of the women sitting cross-legged on each side of the drum, beating out a heart-quickening rhythm with the flat of their hands, the men and boys began to chant in earnest. The wild and vigorous voices soared and swooped and flew into the night.

I felt the drumbeat pounding along my bloodstream.

Amodi's uncle still danced his high-stepping dance, moving around his slow-motion circle. Was he really possessed? Was he truly not conscious of what he was doing? I had the strange feeling that it was a performance, that he was conscious of his audience. It was choreographed and controlled.

I had seen spirit possession before, in Nigeria, the fully-fledged version where women of the *bori* cult were grotesquely possessed by the spirits of gods and animals, thrown into violent contortions and facial grimaces. This was quite different, this stately tranced dance.

A hand tugged at my shirt-sleeve. Tsalert, Amodi's mother, smiled up at me.

I couldn't smile back. I was becoming aware of a crawling sensation in the flesh. I was angry. Inexplicably, angry.

I studied the possessed man again as my heart thudded to the drumbeat. What the fuck was wrong with me? Then a woman threw herself suddenly into the circle in violent dance. This was different again – a frenetic, orgiastic shaking of breasts and hips.

"The spirits have caught her too!" shouted Chimbizat.

Two women darted forward. One removed the huge silver earrings which swung crazily from the dancer's elongated lobes, while the other fumbled at her back. As I saw the baby being lifted from the mother's back – the ecstatic face of the mother, the fat little startled face of the baby, the two other faces intent on a familiar task – I thought for the first time of the camera around my neck. I must record this. But I couldn't. I couldn't lift the camera.

I was amazed at the frenzy of the woman. So that was what lay beneath the serene everyday impassivity? But, again, if she was out of conscious control, why didn't she tear or shake her clothes off – why again the certain level of propriety?

It had to be hysteria, not possession.

I couldn't lift the camera. To lift it was to acknowledge this spectacle, in a sense to accept it. I stood there frozen, unable to make the commitment.

At my side, Amodi's mother fell to the ground like a stone and began to roll frenziedly. On the opposite side of the circle a man fell.

I couldn't see Amodi. A powerful revulsion seized me as

if by the throat. I swung away and beat my way through the crowd.

Blindly I strode out of the camp and on over the sand, heart thumping, bursting with rage. I heard a voice call my name but I didn't stop until I was brought to a halt by a hand gripping my shoulder.

And I knew, before I turned, that it was him.

I turned. It was Amodi, *tagilmoust* around his neck, braided hair gleaming in the moonlight, the sword I had bought for him slung on his shoulder.

"Ellen! Are you well?" The dark-golden eyes were wide with concern.

I stared at him, speechless, thoughts darting around in my head. I didn't have the language to tell him. I had nothing to say that would make sense to him.

I didn't even know what was the matter with me.

Here, in the moment when I should have clung to him, when I should have burst with the joy of seeing his face before me, I just stared.

"Sit down," he said in a murmur, pressing me down by the shoulders, and he swung the long sword in its red scabbard from his shoulder.

I unhitched my camera. We sat on the sand, facing each other. I laid my futile camera carefully on my lap.

He was wearing a white open-sided robe, on one side hitched up on his shoulder. I could see the heavy dark-green soapstone bracelet on the upper arm above his elbow, holding a cluster of leather-covered charms in place. His sword-arm. I couldn't for the life of me, in a million years, ever imagine this most gentle of men actually using a sword.

He fell silent. How could he do that? Be silent.

I sat there, helpless, strangling in my Irish need to verbalise but with no clear understanding of my anger and rejection and disgust.

"The man is your uncle?" I forced myself to say eventually.

"Yes," he answered quietly in his light gentle voice. "He just came back to the camp with me. When he saw the Landrobel fear caught him and he fainted to the ground. Until spirits entered him."

He fell silent again. A rich heady smell came from his body and clothes. I inhaled deeply. The smell of the tribe. The smell of their mothers when they were babies at the breast. Could he ever, in his soul, feel at ease with anyone who didn't smell like that?

Here he was, in the flesh. Not a figment of my longing and imagination. But the living, breathing man, here. My eyes ate him up – the mass of braided hair that, with his slim muscled frame, made him seem to me like a lithe Minoan bull-dancer – and yet there was a heavy earthy weight in those muscles that I knew well. Even clothed, his people always seemed naked – moved as if they were – nothing restricting them, moulding them. I could never look at him without seeing the lines of his naked body, the curve of the buttocks, the swing of his penis. His skin was gold-blue. Gold and blue, like an Egyptian statue from a tomb, with the fine nose that formed almost a straight line with the forehead, the slanted almond eyes outlined heavily in kohl under the delicate perfect arch of the brows and the generously moulded mouth. But the hands – the hands were small and square and endearing – you looked at his hands with their square-tipped fingers and felt the body housed a childlike spirit dressed in an adult's clothes. You wanted to take all the clothes away and let him run free. I thought of the time we had travelled thousands of miles to the south of Nigeria – I was trying to renew my passport in Lagos. We had gone to Bar Beach – and no, they weren't holding any executions there that day, no rattle of bullets or bound bodies – and Amodi had thrown off his clothes and stood in the boiling waves with their powerful dangerous undertow. Ataka, Ilyas and Haruna had joined him, holding hands one behind the other, forming a line of elated defiance against the waves. I remembered Amodi most – buttocks tensed, braids and genitals swinging, left hand reaching out to the pounding waves while he laughed defiance. None of them had ever seen the sea before.

Now I wanted to reach out and touch those hands that I loved but I didn't move.

"Is it fear you are feeling?" he asked at last, softly.

Yes, that was simple and right. That made sense. "Yes," I said. "Especially when I saw your mother."

"It is nothing," he said. "They enter her easily. She will find ease."

We sat in silence. I began to calm. The drum thudded in the background.

"You know," he said finally, raising that index finger against the side of his mouth. The voice was soft and measured – a tone and attitude I recognised. There was going to be a revelation after all. "When I was young I had spirits with me. They were troubling me greatly. *Greatly*. Until a certain *mallam* took me with him into the desert and kept me there for three months. We didn't see anyone all that time. He was giving me medicine all the time until they left me. After that I found my ease from them. Until this day I have my health. So, I too have fear of them."

I thought, would yeh doubt him, to have a good dose of spirits? If there were spirits going, he'd be sure to have them. The only wonder was that he'd given them up.

He began to wind his *tagilmoust* on. I reached out and pulled two glossy plaits out to hang on either side of his face, as I liked them. I ran my hands down them.

"Let's go back," he said.

"No, I don't want to." Panic. Did he not want me at all?

"To your sleeping-place. They will drum all night – by now the spirits will have entered many."

Great. When one's mother's possessed it's OK to sleep with the girlfriend.

And then, on the hard surface of the woven mat on the wooden bed, I had once more my heart's desire, feeling once more in the darkness the solid weight of him, the heavy silky braids of hair, the silky heavy penis, the smoothly muscled body, the silky curves of the buttocks. There was always a perfection in our coupling, a sweet melding that never asked for much movement, a squeezing grasping heavy cleaving that didn't allow all those brief little departures and returns of normal intercourse – the teasing go and come – with Amodi it was as if slotting together were all the act called for.

And this time, I visualised my child.

Later as we lay together and I held him and touched him

and kissed his sleeping skin, and listened to the drumbeat, I stared into the darkness until my thoughts began to get a sharp clear edge.

What had angered me so much about the possession?

And why, as usual, no pictures? I couldn't be single-minded about making a record. Making hay wasn't really my priority. I was in love. My emotional bonds were making me blunder about. I needed a cool photographer's eye. I had a cool photographer's eye and it constantly saw startling beautiful images but I would never capture the drama of the culture until I cleared out the great hot mess in my heart that made me shy away when I should be zooming in.

But the possession . . .

They were so . . . they pandared to the experience, pandared to the spirits. Rushed to get the drum. Fell like stones.

Kept no rational control.

I resented it, resented them their capacity for celebration, for release, for community. Especially that. The powerful bond of community that led them so cheerfully to pandar to the hysteria of one of their number.

That shut me out.

I was jealous. Fiercely jealous.

And, I feared for them. Feared the inbred self-absorption that would be the death of them. The game of survival had changed its parameters and they were still playing by the old rules. They were ostriches with their heads in the sand. And the enemy was all around.

I thought of our life together in Zaria, the fun, the laughter of it.

But he, as much as I, could only be himself and free

when an emigrant away from the stranglehold of family and belief.

Here was a web, a net of such density I had no hope of cutting it.

Then, staring at the goatskin roof, listening to the unrelenting drum, I wondered why I hadn't asked him why he had not returned to Zaria and me.

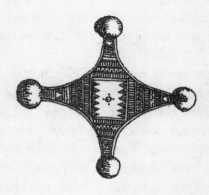

# Chapter 9

Maryam was squatting at the mouth of the tent. "*Maymos etus wah?*" she said shrilly. *What kind of sleep is this?* It was late. Maybe eight o'clock.

Amodi rose sleepily and sheepishly and ducked out of the tent, adjusting his *tagilmoust*.

Maryam shuffled in, squatting. She surveyed me, her rather mannishly handsome features bland.

Goddammit. I hated this! Christ, you didn't need much

wit or cross-cultural perceptions to know that a woman needed to straighten her clothes out and have a pee before having guests of a morning!

This is what annoyed me more than anything, the failure to treat me like an ordinary human being with human reactions. As if, somehow, I didn't have to urinate or clean up after sex or blow my nose.

I sat up and fumbled at my wrapper but didn't have the confidence to navigate the squat-and-duck manoeuvre necessary to exit under the low-hanging leather of the tent, in front of her, with my clothes in God knows what insecure state.

Could she smell the sex off me? She must do.

"You don't have a wrapper to give me?" she asked with the faintest whine of complaint in her rather harsh voice.

Oh, Christ, not before I had an early-morning pee! I was weary of all the begging. What could I say? They'd leave me with nothing. I pulled the dark pink one with the black pattern imposed out of the mouth of my bag and proffered it without ceremony. She took it without the slightest show of enthusiasm and slung it over a tent-rope over her head. No thanks. Nor did she leave.

"Have you not finished with those tins?" she asked, indicating my two NIDO milk tins.

"Yes, I've finished with one." I would need the other to house my camera on the way back.

I reached over and passed it to her, whereupon she raised the tent flap and shrilled, "Come!"

A moment later the extraordinary figure of a Wodaabe woman was squatting there on her lean legs as she enthusiastically examined the tin.

I examined her. I counted eight huge metal hoops, with little amber pieces attached, piercing the whole perimeter of each ear – not just the lobes. Her neck was festooned with large amber beads and strings of tiny leather and brass charms like little round pods, her face delicately traced with blue tattooed lines, the characteristic round bunch of hair projecting over her forehead. She was wearing a short tight little wrapper about her lean hips and a little top that barely covered the upper half of her neat breasts leaving the lower half bare. She would have looked at home hanging out with a gang of fashion-conscious punks at Piccadilly Circus. I marvelled again at the dramatic difference between these neighbours, the Wodaabe all lean sinew, the Tuareg all opulent curves.

She was plainly excited about my NIDO tin. Why? Why would she need a tin when she no doubt owned a dozen calabashes? As a butterchurn?

Djanetta ducked under the tent-leather with Yassine's Raechitu on her back. "Ellen! How was your sleep?"

I smiled. "All is well!" I was glad to see her.

"Look," said Maryam in Tamajegh, indicating the wrapper slung on the tent rope above her with the tiniest pointing movement of the lips.

"Did the *Takafart* give you that?" asked Djanetta.

"Yes." She turned her head a little and glanced at it disdainfully. "It's not beautiful."

"No," agreed Djanetta with a grimace. "It's not beautiful."

I went hot with rage. Goddammit. I needed the bloody wrapper. I was down to three now. Why had I given it to her? And why did they assume I didn't understand Tamajegh when it should be clear to any idiot that I did? And the double insult of the casual reference to me as the *Takafart*.

Some sort of discussion or bartering with the Wodaabe was proceeding. Maryam was bargaining for a set of three huge darning-needles, it appeared. In exchange for the NIDO tin? My irritation about the wrapper gave me the nerve to jump into this unclear situation – something I normally would never do. I grabbed up the NIDO tin and thrust it into the Wodaabe woman's hands, saying in Hausa, "I give it to you!" with emphatic giving hand-gestures to back that up.

Before I had the time, or the nerve, to look and see how Maryam had taken that, a chattering of female voices sounded and a bunch of Arab women emerged through the circle of thorn trees. They were draped head to foot in dusty black-blue cotton and had little of the evident dramatic beauty of the Tuareg – at least to my eye which maybe by this time saw through Tuareg lens. While not veiled, they kept their faces covered by pulling some of their trailing cotton veiling across their faces with a hand. They came and bent and greeted the women and stared at me, raising hands in salute.

Maryam began to speak to them in Arabic.

It intrigued me when they clustered about the Land Cruiser, marvelling at it, examining everything, looking in the side-mirror, staring in with hands pressed flat against the glass, giggling and exclaiming. It was only then it struck me that the Tuareg women in the camp had never deigned to get up off their backsides and examine the car. Their goddamn pride and self-sufficiency. God, they were so *proud*. They had behaved as if the car simply wasn't there or like European suburban housewives with a car or two parked as a matter of course outside the door.

The Wodaabe woman was clutching my NIDO tin, still with her set of needles in her hand. It pleased and amused me that she had eyes only for what made sense in her world. Not a Landrover, not even a cotton wrapper – for her a milk-container was the pearl without price.

She thanked me profusely over and over and I smiled and smiled until I thought my face would break, still dying for a pee and desperate for Haruna to arrive so that I could beg for the one and only thing that made sense in my world at this time in the morning: a cup of ordinary sugarless Indian tea.

Finally, while the others were still distracted by the activities around the car I struggled out of the tent and, clutching my toilet roll, set off for the nearest sand-dune.

Then, to my intense annoyance, I saw the three lads – Haruna, Ilyas and Sideka – following me. For Christ's sake!

"*Madame! Madame!*" they shouted in giggling parody of the daily cat-calls from kids and others.

I waited, vexed.

"In the name of God, will you not let me go piss?"

"Hey! Your man is waiting for you behind that hill," said Haruna. "Are you two trying to hide from us?"

And sure enough, when we topped the hill, there was Amodi squatting in the sand in the process of relieving himself. The lads began to hoot and holler and tore down to run rings around Amodi while I followed.

"Come here! Come here, darling!" called Amodi sweetly, using the English endearment he knew from me.

"What for?" I asked.

"Come! Come!" he signalled me to come to where he squatted.

I went over to him, grinning but uncertain, while the three lads ran back hooting to a safe distance.

"Sit down, sit down," he said in English.

I squatted in front of him. His heavy black baggy trousers were bunched around his knees and his white robe pulled up behind around his waist.

"Now give me a kiss," he said wickedly. And he pursed his lips like a child.

Laughing and amazed at such a bizarre notion, I kissed him, while the three lads threw themselves around in the sand in laughter.

"God bless you, Amodi!" said Ilyas finally and quite soberly. "You are a true madman!"

I made my way back to the camp giggling, with my heart singing.

More than anything Amodi had ever said or done, that zany act made my heart beat fast in hope for the future. In that act he had allied himself to a whole world outside his desert and that zany streak might be our salvation. That capacity to step outside the conventions.

I didn't dwell on the fact that he had done it only in front of the boys, the lads he shared that life on another planet with.

# Chapter 10

With Ilyas, I went to look for Kulutan. Eventually we found him lounging under an acacia tree, lazily playing a reed flute. He glanced up at us quizzically and continued to play, letting us settle and wait. The notes warbled hauntingly in a minor key, the sound liquid in the dryness, like a race memory of running streams.

He was bareheaded so I could see his face. Smiling, I looked at him and waited. We were good friends, with a solid affection between us.

Three years before he had asked me to let him live with

me. He had explained that he had thought it all out. He had no herds of his own in Niger, he wanted to settle in Nigeria, he could pass as a black African unlike the others, he could fit into Nigerian society. If I invested some money in him – got him a licence and bought a taxi for instance, he would build up a business for us and wouldn't hanker to go back to Niger where he was just a slave. And, by the way, he was in love with me.

All this was absolutely correct. I knew it made sense. But I also knew that for me to live with a "slave" would be such a breach of Tuareg values that they would almost certainly write me off – ostracise me from the culture that fascinated me.

The fact that I would be also ostracised, or as good as, from European society didn't enter unduly into my calculations.

But then, in any case, I met and fell in love with Amodi.

Kulutan stopped playing and smiled his beautiful smile, laughingly and lazily greeting Ilyas. "Brother!"

And I remembered then that the use of the word "brother" wasn't casual: Kulutan belonged to Ilyas's family. Captured in raids on caravans crossing the desert or bought in Agadez or slave markets to the south, the Iklan were black Africans who were absorbed into the culture and became the fictive children of their masters – the master was their "father" and mistress their "mother" and slave and free children grew up together forming the bonds of family. Aghali was Kulutan's fictive father and so Ilyas was his brother.

"Mister Kulutan!" said Ilyas in English – a recognition of their different relationship in Nigeria. "When did you come here?"

"We thought you were still in Nigeria," I said. He had left Zaria some months before to look for work in Kano and we had lost contact.

"Madame Ellen!" Kulutan pulled his hand through mine, flicking at my fingers. "I came here only one month ago."

He began to play again in a desultory fashion, strong graceful brown-black hands poised as he fingered the notes, sculpted lips delicately tensed as he blew the pipe. He was a gorgeous man, well-muscled yet supple, the strong lines of his wonderful profile emphasised by a few inches of beard. In Zaria he had at one time taken to wearing a green army beret, which had me fantasising for a while on Kulutan dressed in green combats playing some kind of Che Guevara role.

I still found him goddam sexy.

How could such a man end up as a slave?

And accepting it.

He had none of my profound emotional problems with the notion of a slave system: his people were stronger than their masters and their black skin could take the sun where fairer skins would burn up – so it was quite proper that they should do the hard work in the sun. Fairer skin was more beautiful than his – his had no brightness.

He had often patiently explained the slave system, past and present, to me, offering grass-roots confirmation of what the textbooks said: that in practice it was a fairly benevolent set-up. The slaves shared the same conditions and lifestyle as the others. If there was no intermarriage, well, neither was there marriage between the other groups in Tuareg society nor indeed between the various ethnic groups in the area. And, as with the craftspeople caste, the Inaden, the feudal system of *noblesse oblige* was in full swing. I knew this to my cost: even in Zaria, if an Akli from Amodi's family made any reasonable demand for food or money or clothing I had to meet it unquestioningly.

The warbling minor notes stopped abruptly in the middle of a phrase. Kulutan looked at me. "You come to take me home?" he asked in English with gentle mockery and a faint giggle that was characteristic.

"Do you want to go?" I asked smiling, not knowing how else to respond.

"Yes," he answered in Tamajegh, the face suddenly almost grave, "I am lonely for you."

Ilyas whooped with laughter.

I hung my head and felt myself blush. And wondered what Ilyas would make of that.


I was sitting in front of Maryam's tent with Yassine, listening to the pleasant hollow sound of the evening grain being pounded. As I sat there a black woman came along, one of the slave caste, big-boned, handsome, with a little boy. He was large-boned like her, a handsome child, with a Mohawk haircut and the usual array of protective charms hung about his hips and and arms and neck. I couldn't judge his age but he was as big as many a five-year-old. I was startled and disturbed when, kneeling beside her, he grabbed one of her elongated breasts in his fist, kneading it expertly, and, eyes riveted on me, raised it to his mouth and began to suckle. I could never get over my European-bred reaction to this. I thought of A'isha milking Yassine's breast. Rationalise my repugnance as I might, the truth was I didn't understand why I found it disturbing – even sexually disturbing. My reaction was the usual tangled web of emotions, and envy and longing for a child of my own heightened my resentment of their complacency in the act.

The child was still staring, fascinated, at me, milk seeping out at the corners of his mouth. He pulled the nipple out for a moment, gazed at me solemnly, then thrust it in again. How *old* was this child?

A desire to find out his age made me clumsily say "How big he is!"

The mother started and muttered something to the others, and without even stopping to free her breast rose immediately to her feet, grabbing up the still-suckling boy, slung him on her hip and hurried away.

I knew, before they told me, what had happened and I blushed with shame.

"She thinks you put a curse on her child – saying he is big – but I told her you didn't mean anything," said Yassine earnestly.

"*Kai!* I forgot. In my country it isn't any harm to say that," I said, knowing that even that was a half-truth. Down in West Cork or out on the islands they still believed in the Evil Eye. She was anxious to comfort me. "It's nothing! Don't worry! I will speak to her again and tell her!"

Jesus. Great. I'd be getting a reputation as a witch.

West Cork, yes. I remembered going out jogging on Cape Clear, off the coast of West Cork, on a dirt road along by the sea and a woman stopping me on the road and saying cheerily, "Your hair is beautiful but I nearly turned back when I saw you – 'tis very bad luck to meet a red-haired woman coming against you on the road!"

I might have thought she was having me on but that evening I saw what I thought was the same woman, smiling across at me in a pub, and it turned out to be the first one's sister.

"You're the girl," she said, "that my sister met this morning. Sure didn't she come straight to tell me!"

I was, to my astonishment, the talk of the island.

"But, tell me, did she spit at you?" she asked.

"Did she *what?*"

"Did she spit at you? She told me that she did – 'tis the only cure, you know!"

"Well, if she did, it must have been at my back when I passed!" I said, hugely pleased at this bizarre idea.

No, I wasn't in much of a position to scorn the Tuareg reaction.

There was nothing quite like the pleasure they had in giving, particularly in sharing food. When I gathered around the big wooden bowl with the other women and we passed the deeply curved wooden spoon from one to the other, they exhorted me all the time to eat, to eat more, eat. The grain and warm fresh milk was very insipid – and unfortunately a great laxative – and it was difficult to appear enthusiastic. I did like it when it was served with fermented yoghurt – that had a bit of a zing. It was beyond all imagination to understand that these women had hardly eaten another thing from birth to death – the occasional bit of meat, an insipid tough dried cheese, some berries in season. That was it.

And the result was: glossy hair, fine teeth, perfect skin. There had to be something wrong with Western theories of diet and Vitamin C. I couldn't see that they got any Vitamin C at all, except whatever residual bit there is in milk. On the other hand, there were many cases of night blindness – something a few carrots could cure.

Another bunch of facts I couldn't sort out.

Before Amodi came, I had been having great fun – and getting a sunburnt nose – larking about with Ilyas on a couple of donkeys. It took some getting used to, the *trit-trot* none too pleasant under you, the back knobbly and unyielding, the after-effects of the friction none too pleasant. But we did manage to get to the well on them a few days.

Then Amodi gave me a camel for my use. I was used to riding – I rode my horse Hadari every day in Zaria tearing around the bush there – and I had ridden camels on previous visits, to the muted dismay of the older women – you could read it in their faces: *no good will come of this*. But the men had taken to the notion of teaching me with great excitement and enthusiasm and were stridently proud when I managed to learn to race along the flat. In fact, the riding in the saddle was the easy part – I had ridden a bolting horse on two occasions in Zaria and managed to keep my seat – but mounting and dismounting was another matter. The Tuareg saddle was a delicate-looking construction which fitted on top of the hump. Behind was a little back-rest, in front a three-pronged pommel. The camel knelt, you perched on this narrow little construction, placed your feet on the neck of the camel and hoped to keep your balance as he lunged to his feet. I was more terrified at the notion of falling off and losing face than I was at the thought of hurting myself.

One morning we awoke to dust and cold. The *harmattan* was upon us, obscuring the sun until mid-morning. I was glad of the thick wraparound cardigan and heavy headscarf I had brought and guiltily watched the naked little kids as I sipped my morning tea. Did they not feel it, the cold?

Against a background of dull *harmattan* dust I took some pictures of Amodi with his little cousin, a gap-toothed thin naked little angel of about six years old with a wild halo of dust-laden hair like Muhane's before Haruna and I had got to work on her. The contrast between the heavily robed and turbaned man and the bare little dusty boy was interesting. The little boy smiled in delight at me but Amodi's eyes were on him. Amodi squatted down and pulled the boy close, embracing him, a hand stroking his dusty skin. I couldn't understand how such evident affection didn't extend to giving him a piece of cloth to wrap up in. Maybe the reason was nothing complicated after all – such as the Evil Eye or my other speculations. Maybe they wanted the children to become tough and hardy and inured to the harsh weather.

Late that night, pressed blissfully against the curve of Amodi's buttocks as he slept, I pondered on the fact that I hadn't simply asked Amodi – or anyone – why they left the children naked in the cold; and I realised I had learned not to bother to ask questions – I had no use for surface answers, the received or taught responses they could all trot out so glibly. Better to watch and try to get under that surface instead.

The well was where it was at. There the normally serene

men became possessed with a surging excitement. Snorting Tuareg camels and big-horned Wodaabe cattle jostled for position while the donkeys or oxen on pulley-duty were exhorted with high-pitched cries of encouragement and every skin of water drawn was greeted by whoops of triumph. This was the business of the desert and its central miracle: when the heavy leather skin of cool water, drawn by rope and pulley and labouring animal from the deeps of the desert, is brought to the glaring surface for a brief mating with the sun before being sucked greedily into the throbbing bodies of camel or man. That supreme moment of coupling living flesh with water. *Aman* was the word for water. *Aman*, two urgently basic syllables – like *Ana* the word they used for "mother" – or *alam* for "camel".

At the well I always became infected by the excitement myself and took photographs with reckless disregard for my small stock of film.

We went there often. On one particular day I wandered off into the harsh dry jumble of trees and scrub around the area. Some teenagers were sitting ahead on the white sand, arranged in a pattern like an emblem of courtship. I sat on a fallen tree-trunk and watched them. Boys faced girls, each group in a V-shaped defensive position, as clear as if it had been drawn in a diagram, each with a natural leader who sat in front. The two leaders faced each other, a couple of yards apart.

To the right of the girl's group and a little way back was a girl who could have made the cover of *Vogue* – a striking contemporary face with generous lips and a beautiful bone structure. She sat quietly, one knee raised, her elbow propped on it, taking no active part in the flirting and conversation, smiling, fiddling with some stones, playing with the silver bracelets on her slim long-boned wrist. She might have been fourteen years old.

I fumbled for my zoom lens, as my eyes scanned the group. The dominant girl, the leader, sat with her legs folded under her, one arm lying across her lap relaxed, the other with its silver bracelets performing a graceful mime of communication as she talked, her head tilted a little to one side.

I snapped the group and got a close-up of the two leaders as they flirted. Then I concentrated on the *Vogue* girl but eventually came back to the leader, fascinated. The line of the heavy graceful arm, the strength and suppleness of the fingers, the great curve of her thighs and buttocks under the black cloth, the white smile flashing from the rounded face. Glowing with health, eyes and hair glistening, skin warm and golden, voice and laughter mellow and rich. Sex personified. And fat, really fat. The young men were all agog.

Suddenly, before I had time to take a picture, the group broke up, the fat girl rising in one surging movement like a powerful animal.

We sat facing each other on the sand, clasping hands, noses pressed together, inhaling each other's breath in the Tuareg way.

But my heart was racing along a different track. I had yet to ask him about leaving for Zaria. If we were to leave.

*Now*, I thought. *Now*.

I squeezed his hands and we kissed again. *Now*. I freed my hand and ran it down one of his glossy plaits. *Now*.

"Amodi, you know . . . I have to go back to Zaria quickly. I have work."

He pulled back a little and the golden-brown eyes were cast down.

Oh Christ, no. Not the silent treatment.

I blundered on. "Why didn't you come before?" I asked with difficulty, not looking in his face. *Why can't I confront people? Why do I back off and give them room to lie?*

He let go my hand. He began to wind on his *tagilmoust*. He adjusted the fold over his mouth, leaving it covered. "I was preparing to come," he said, voice muffled.

"When? When were you coming?"

"You know, I wanted to travel with Sideka. But Aghali had a problem. He is ill. His back is troubling him. You know, all the Iklan have gone to Nigeria and, with Sideka and Ilyas away, Aghali had no one to graze his goats. So we had to wait until Kulutan came – we heard he was coming."

"What is your meaning? If Kulutan came, what then?"

"He would graze the goats and Sideka would be able to go."

I didn't believe it! There must be bunches of kids around who could mind goats! What was this?

"But Kulutan has been here a month! Or so he says! Why didn't you leave?"

"They couldn't agree, he and Sideka, which one should go back to Zaria."

"And now? What will happen?"

"If Kulutan agrees, Sideka will go back to Zaria."

Kulutan *or* Sideka?

"If he agrees?"

"We can't force him."

"And you?" My exasperation gave me the courage to ask.
"I will go."

I didn't believe a word of it. It was the lamest possible story.

He just hadn't come. But the question was: had he intended to come?

No, the question was: would he come now?

What if he wouldn't? What the fuck was I to do? It was simply impossible for me to pick myself up and leave him, now that we were welded together again. I couldn't do it. It couldn't be expected of me. But, Jesus, if I lost my job? Had to return to Ireland? What then? If he didn't come soon, I *would* have to find the strength, would have to go.

I began to suffer. I suppose, up to that, I had been hoping that he would have some overwhelmingly convincing excuse for not coming back to me. Yes, probably, they had been fecking about waiting on this and that, waiting for each other – maybe Sideka's indecision was the problem. Their concepts of time were vague and flexible in any case. While I was counting off days on a calendar, he would be waiting for the next new moon or the next season. But, for all such rationalisations, the stark fact was that he hadn't cared enough, hadn't felt any of my desperate need to be with him.

It was a blow to find that there had been nothing in particular to prevent him coming; and it was cruelly hard in that situation, with no private space, on a public platform as I was. There was no area to retreat to – except inside my brain – and even when I retreated to that tortured space I could never rid myself of the mask. I could never cry or

frown or show anger or despair. I could only turn my back at
night and weep silently into the darkness.

Yes, I thought once again, I needed a black Tuareg veil
such as the men had, which masked all things except
dignity, or the great black enveloping veil of the women
that could mask any sorrow.

I was sharing some meat with little Raechitu and Muhane.
Raechitu trembled visibly as I cut her a piece, so starved was
she for protein.

"She's like a cat!" said Amodi laughing. "Look at her
body, how it dances!"

They thought it funny; I thought it obscene and it cut me
to the heart. "She's hungry," I said in pain. "She needs
meat." I had fed her all the powdered milk in my remaining
NIDO tin, so now my camera lay exposed with no hiding-
place for the return journey.

"But Ellen is full of love for children!" said Djanetta
emotionally. Then she suddenly rose to her feet. "Come!
Come!" she said, as always gesturing emphatically. I got up
clumsily – it was impossible to resist her energy – and,
picking little Raechitu up, I followed her with Muhane
scampering at my heels.

Amodi came too, rising from his cross-legged position in
the same one powerful graceful movement I had seen the
girl use at the well, like a sleight of hand my eye couldn't
register.

Djanetta plodded ahead, arm gracefully urging me on,
her prominent buttocks bouncing, black wrapper trailing in
the dust. She led the way to a tent I hadn't visited before,
squatting and shuffling in a duck-like waddle under the low

leather overhang of the entrance, leaving me to awkwardly crouch and stumble in, carrying Raechitu. At first glance the tent was empty.

"Look!" she said, her features smiling but with the usual lively light absent. "My boy."

In a shallow depression in the sand lay a dusty naked little boy of about five years old, clutching at a cloth wrapper, stick-like legs drawn up to his stomach, chin raised unnaturally.

I was astonished. Why hadn't she shown him before? And why so cheerfully and casually now?

"Salach, Salach!" she said, stroking his back.

Amodi had come in. He moved forward and squatted in front of the boy and reaching out took the slim little hand and gave it the traditional stroking handshake. The little boy reared his shaven head and swayed from side to side.

"He doesn't see," said his mother, pointing index and middle finger to her own eyes. And I saw his eyes were milky white and rolled back in his head.

But he was responding to Amodi, grinning joyfully at his touch.

"How are you, Salach?" said Amodi. "Poor thing – look, he feels pleasure. Salach! Salach!" He sat back and took the child in his arms. "Salach!"

"Careful he doesn't make shit on you!" said his mother quickly, grabbing up the cloth and bunching it under the child's little buttocks.

Jesus, I thought, what if this child is only physically retarded? What if a full intelligence is trapped in there?

"Look," said Djanetta in Tamajegh, pointing the lips at me. "She is worrying. She feels pity for him." She broke into

Hausa and her voice rose into a more emphatic public tone. "Amodi! You must force Ellen to stay here with us!"

Amodi stroked the little shaven head and said nothing.

"Stay until you become beautiful like Aminatu!" Djanetta cried at me. The old theme. *"Big!"* She slapped a supple forefinger energetically on her palm, almost bending it right backwards, and drew it through a fist, in the familiar gesture for "beautiful".

"Aminatu?"

"A beautiful woman! *To,*" she raised a finger and eagerly began to tell one of her stories – by now I had realised she was a gifted storyteller. "Listen. Before, there was a woman in Tillia, her name was Aminatu, and news of her was heard everywhere she was so beautiful. And she was so big she had to be carried about!" Her cheeks puffed out and the arms made the usual circle. "She couldn't walk at all! *To!* One day they carried her to the well to wash – they had to wash her, you know – she couldn't wash herself – she couldn't touch behind. At all, at all! Because she was so fat! And when she took off her things, she took her earrings and put them *here* – " a hand thrust into the fold between her thigh and her heavy belly " – for safe keeping. And afterwards she forgot where she put them! They searched and searched everywhere!" She mimed the searching in the sand. "But they couldn't find them! Until she found them two months after, still where she had put them, when they began to chafe her skin! She had such a body!"

Her face was alight with the delight of it. Amodi's eyes were dancing too.

And I – I hugged Raechitu and smiled.

*She is dazzling harmony,*

*A full, shining moon,*
*Scarred with stretchmarks are her belly and flanks,*
*Vast expanses of exquisite softness . . .*

Amodi was still stroking the little shaven head. I reached out and stroked the thin cheek with the back of my hand.

Solemnly, Muhane put the back of her little hand against Salach's other cheek, copying me.

"You know, the spirits did this," said Amodi.

"How?"

"They stole him – he's a changeling."

"He had his health when he was born," said Djanetta ruefully. She made a little sound of annoyance and regret. "You know, sometimes the spirits do that – they steal a child and put one of their own instead."

I stared, perplexed. What were they saying? The spirits did this to *him* – he had *his* health when *he* was born – ? *He* is a changeling? Was this a spirit child or Djanetta's?

Afterwards we left Djanetta and went in the evening cool to milk the camels. He pulled his *tagilmoust* down around his neck and got to work. As he stood leaning his head against the flank of the animal and I held the wooden bowl for the milking, I asked him – with effort and studied casualness. "Didn't I hear that if a child is deformed at birth some people kill it?"

"Yes, that is done."

"Or if the woman isn't married?"

"Yes."

"How?" My voice was a whisper.

He didn't answer immediately. I kept quiet.

"They give birth into a hole and cover them," he said quietly.

"Truly?"

"Truly."

"Who?"

"The women."

"Do many of them do that?"

He stopped milking and, looking not at me but at the flank of the camel, raised a finger in pronouncement. "It would be hard to find one who doesn't do it."

There was condemnation in his voice. To him, it was outside him. Something the women do. Are obliged to do because they whore around.

All my hackles rose. And I was a hair's breadth away from anger again. With the culture. With the women. With the men. With *him*.

"So Salach wasn't born like that? And if he had been born like that – he would have been killed?" *Djanetta* would have killed him?

"Without a doubt."

My soul sighed. I watched and heard the fizzing of the milk into the wooden bowl.

"Who was Salach's father?" I asked after a while.

"He is from Tillia. He divorced her after Salach's birth."

So – someone outside the family gene-pool. I had asked because I wondered whether Salach's condition had anything to do with the constant inbreeding they practised. I vaguely thought – convulsions of some kind, epilepsy? I knew they favoured marriage with their first cousins because of the matrilineal system – it meant that the man's children would have rights of inheritance and succession within the family group – otherwise his children would belong to their mother's family, outside the group.

One had only to look at the people of this area, the fair skin and straight hair, the Mediterranean features, to see how they, even more than other Tuareg groups, had systematically inbred over the centuries. Surrounded by black ethnic groups, living side by side with them and intimately with their own Inaden and Iklan, they had never stepped out of line and intermarried or interbred. Maybe that was why they had such a fierce insistence on their narrow standards of beauty – maybe it was sheer survival of the group as a group. Jesus. Was I to end up condoning racism? I leant my head wearily next to Amodi's against the flank of the camel. And I felt a million miles away from the world inside the sleek blue-black head beside my own.

# Chapter 11

A taka was making me a ring. His little anvil set in its block of wood was standing at the ready and, in a little depression in the sand, his charcoals were glowing. Tools of the trade were scattered around: tongs, hammer, files, chisels, a little bellows. An empty can full of water for cooling.

A blackened pot full of charcoal. Blocks of wood with various grooves in them for moulding pieces of metal into little bars. Flat cakes of beeswax.

I had bought the requisite Maria Theresa taler in Agadez. The great silver coin with the head of the Austrian Empress was still minted somewhere or other for just this purpose: it was always the base for silver jewellery.

In the hyperbole of song, Sharibu buys three talers to have a ring made . . .

*Sharibu bought three silver coins to make a ring,*
*He wears the finest decorations on his tagilmoust . . .*

One would have to suffice for me.

*Sharibu is tall and straight like a palm-tree next to a wall,*
*May all news of him be good!*
*I want Sharibu,*
*My heart is shredded,*
*My heart is like a tarred road with cars going over it,*
*I'm not ashamed to say I want him,*
*I won't keep quiet about it . . .*

Shredded. A good word, shredded.

I tried to concentrate on Ataka.

Ataka's people were a special caste, simultaneously disdained and respected by the Tuareg nobility. A craftsman could make quite outrageous demands on his superior – for instance, there were musicians among them who could arrive with their entourage and live off a patron for some time, expecting also a big gift in money or kind on their departure. They were often poets and singers, with a satirical bent which could be stimulated by any poor treatment and so a craftsman had to be well treated at all costs. Exactly the same as in our Irish bardic tradition, in fact.

Ataka had modelled my ring in wax the day before, covered it in a clay paste and left it to dry. It would have the typical rectangular raised frontispiece which would have a decorative pattern and little vertical grooves into which he would insert some slivers of black stone.

He then lightly fired the clay that housed the wax model and poured the melted wax out into the can of water where it hardened for future use, repeating this until all the wax was well and truly out. He had melted my silver coin in a little clay crucible buried in the charcoal and then, with the tongs, had taken it out and poured it into the waiting clay mould. And again waited for it to cool.

What skill! And what a place it ensured for them in this society where jewellery and weapons of war were the objects of desire. Metalwork must seem magical in a pre-technological society – in any case, the man with the craft to forge one's weapons of war is a man to be nurtured, feared and respected.

Now Ataka shattered the little crucible and my ring was born, covered with a layer of oxidation, a rough sulphur-yellow without shine.

"I thank God," he said, grinning. It was perfect. No flaws.

Now he could get to work with a will, with chisel and file and sand and a little steel burin that he sharpened constantly.

Like the tea-ceremony, it lulled the soul to sit cross-legged and watch him work – utterly concentrated, utterly relaxed – for an entire morning or afternoon or day – indeed, days, if he were working on a knife or sword.

There could be no hurry, no haste, it would be ready when it was ready, finished when it was finished. Time was not a factor.

Today, however, our peace was broken when a bunch of

people gathered to watch and chat and eventually launched into raucous play.

Maryam was joking with Ikus-Ikoos, her first cousin, in the outrageous way that first cousins – playmates who had a "joking relationship" – were allowed to do by custom. He was lying in her lap while she searched for lice in his hair and she was making a huge performance out of each catch. Lice-hunting was a regular part of life here. Every louse and nit she captured was held aloft while she uttered wild curses on them before crunching them audibly between her fingernails.

"Was there ever a louse like this one? Look how fat, how lazy, how stupid, how easy to catch it is! Just like its master! He has a louse-farm in his head! He feeds them on oil and butter! Look at it! Big enough to feed the whole camp! Boys, prepare the fire! We must roast this for the evening meal!"

"In the name of God, woman, shut up and do your job! As if anyone would eat a louse killed by you, a worthless dirty woman, without a knife or prayer!"

"Wait, wait, until I get enough to pound for porridge – hah, slave-girl, go get your mortar and pestle!"

"*Kai*, get your hands off my head, woman! Leave my lice alone! They are my brothers! We live well together!" He pulled away from her.

"By the Will of God!" cried Maryam with a big stagey show of horror. "Ellen, did you hear that! A fart! Did you hear the fart that this bastard just made?"

"By God, *I* did!" said Sideka. "But I think it was this worthless slave here!" Meaning, of course, Haruna, whose favourite party-trick was farting at will to the delight of any assembly. I could never figure out the business about farting

– something which was at the same time seriously offensive and wildly hilarious. It was the biggest joke in the world and they all fell around like schoolboys when it happened and yet it was regarded as the most appalling of social gaffes.

"Let me see if I have any!" said Haruna, and he thrust his buttocks in the air and had a go to no avail.

"No, no, it was this fool here! Let me punish him!" said Maryam and she began to grab up pieces of Ataka's red-hot charcoal, in the confident way they had of handling fire, attempting to burn Ikus-Ikoos's bare shins with them. He kicked the pieces away but then she did burn him and he sprang to his feet with a roar.

*"In the name of God, woman, you are a she-devil!"* and he began to pantomime trampling her with his bare feet.

*"You're the devil!"* shouted Maryam and, reaching up, grabbed his genitals through the bunched cotton of his trousers. She opened her mouth wide, with its serious-looking set of large white teeth, and made great play of trying to close it on the handful of genitals while he belaboured her with a sandal. For a horrific few moments I thought she actually might bite his prick or balls off because the only rule between "playmates" was that anything was allowed and could not be punished or avenged. My hair stood on end as she actually stuffed some of the handful in her mouth but then she drew back spitting and grabbed Sideka by the hair. "Sideka! Boy! Come and help me! Here! You bite him for me!"

And the play broke up in laughter as she pressed the bunch of cloth and flesh into Sideka's open mouth.

Ikus-Ikoos landed a mighty blow on her head with the sandal and she let go of him and Sideka.

She sat back gasping and uttering threats and curses while he beat a retreat clutching his genitals and then suddenly, still gasping, she caught me by the arm and pointed. "Look," she said. "There! Do you see that girl?"

I looked. A slim young girl was squatting at the mouth of the opposite tent, shaking a goatskin of milk back and forth – making butter. It was the *Vogue* girl. She smiled broadly as she saw us looking.

"That is Amodi's wife!" said Maryam.

My world lurched, a house of cards collapsing. "What do you mean?" I asked, my voice remote and casual.

"She is his first cousin – the daughter of his aunt. She's his wife!"

I said nothing. I asked nothing. I didn't want to know. I didn't know if they were teasing me, trying to take a rise out of me as we would say at home. It could indeed be one of their jokes. Or it could be true. There could be a marriage arranged; it was the custom. It wouldn't necessarily mean they were actually married yet – wouldn't necessarily mean it would ever happen.

I should ask. Why not ask? Jesus, I was becoming so Tuareg I was almost impassive.

Why not ask a simple question now? Even if it did make me appear a fool, falling for a sly joke. But, what good would asking do me? The answer would be "yes", wouldn't it? Even if it was a joke, or even if the arrangement amounted to no more than some laughing exchanges between the girl's father and his around the campfire when they were infants.

It was happening now with some frequency. But oddly,

usually with the men. I would approach a group and they would fall silent, muttering in their *tagilmousts*, greeting me with a hearty cheerfulness that left a watchful look in their eyes.

I began to imagine they were gossiping about me and Amodi. Since the mention of his "wife" I was becoming increasingly paranoiac and had begun to notice his frequent absences. But, in that case, if it were gossip, why the men and not the women? That puzzled me. Could it be that they knew something about Amodi that the women didn't?

A few times, when I joined them, the talk would start up again but then it was usually some talk of politics as they understood them: largely to do with Gaddafi's attempts to lure Tuaregs into his special battalions in Libya with promises of a Central Saharan Republic straddling northern Niger and Chad and southern Algeria and Libya.

There were always rumours and gossip rife about how perilous or easy it was to cross the border into Libya by foot. While I knew a couple of Tuareg who had actually seen Tripoli – or Trabolis as they called it – and the Mediterranean, I also knew of others attempting to cross the border whose bodies were found in the desert, having died of thirst.

I hated to hear this stuff. I feared so much that Amodi would go. I knew it was a dream they all had. Libya seemed like Paradise to them, a goldmine where one could live in comfort in a government house, work and earn more money than they had ever dreamed of, or join the army and wear a uniform and be paid for the privilege. Luckily, there was one snag that prevented a mass exodus to this Land of Plenty: no women. They reported this in rueful tones. Libya might be the Land of Plenty but it was also the Land of Suffering. How could a Tuareg man live without women? Years without being near a woman? Was that life or death?

One evening after sundown I joined the usual group and spontaneously one of them sat erect and burst into song, the voice with an echoing cleaving tone as if it had a touch of brass or silver in it:

*He saw Hassan coming at a run to shoot him,*
*He was filled with fighting spirit,*
*He shot at Hassan and got him in the neck,*
*The bullet smashed his backbone;*
*He lifted his foot to his knee*
*And resting his elbow on his leg*
*Aimed through the sights . . .*

Later, out on the sand, alone with Amodi, I asked, "That song – the one about Hassan and Akhmed – why were they fighting?"

"To . . . Akhmed was a bandit, an *Elfilayga*. He was hiding from the police in the mountains. You know, when they told us to give up all our guns and weapons, some people hid them in the rocks. They took our spears too and swords."

"But you still wear swords . . . "

"Yes, but it is not really legal. We usually hide them. They can take them if they wish."

"Didn't you need guns for hunting?"

He shrugged. "Yes."

"But who was Hassan?"

"He was a *goumier*, an Akli, a black Buzu."

A *goumier*. A desert policeman.

I couldn't condone it. I put my head down on my raised knees and said nothing.

Their lawlessness would be the death of them. They just didn't see it. Their heads were still in the Middle Ages.

I grimaced to myself. Stupid. The Middle Ages for them was the beginning of the century. In 1881 they had massacred an expedition of almost a hundred Frenchmen in southern Algeria. Eleven of the French survived a 750-mile march back through the desert, resorting to cannibalism, being picked off all the way by the sinister veiled Blue Men.

Looking at Amodi now, I could no more imagine him raiding, slaving or ingratiating himself into a passing caravan only to rise at the dead of night to slit throats than . . . Could I really imagine one of the familiar swords being raised and brought down to slice a hand or an arm off? Yet that was their purpose. And one of my friends had to flee Niger because he had done just that – lopped off someone's hand in a swordfight.

"Ellen?"

I started. He was gazing at me questioningly. I looked at him in anger.

"Why, why can't you people just settle peacefully?" I said, my voice trembling. "Until you draw the anger of the government on you all. They already think half of you are spying for Libya. I'm telling you the day will come when they take you all and lock you up!"

He was taken aback by my outburst.

But then my eyes filled with tears. A mistake.

"El-len! Don't cry!" He took the tail of his *tagilmoust* and tenderly wiped the tears from the corners of my eyes. "Nothing will happen! They won't do anything! If they do we'll beat them!" And he flicked his hand with a snap in the beating gesture.

I hissed in exasperation. But said nothing. What was the point?

He was grinning.

"What?" I said belligerently.

"Your nose is blue."

"Oh!" I laughed.

He took the *tagilmoust* end again and smeared its indigo over my face, smiling. "Now you are beautiful!" And he rubbed noses with me as we lay back on the sand and he loosened the waist-string of his trousers.

# Chapter 12

Kulutan was at the well, among the dry bushes and trees that encircled it. He was squatting naked among some jerrycans, about to wash, when I came upon him. He turned his head and grinned his beautiful grin at me over his shoulder. Unabashed but mischievous. "Ellen!"

I stayed a few yards back and watched him. Pretty unabashed and mischievous myself.

He unended the first jerrycan with a ripple of dark

muscles in arms and back and buttocks. The water gushed over his head and back in a glossy stream condensing into sparkling drops on the dense negroid hair as if it never really penetrated it. Then he threw his head back and, raising both arms, emptied a second jerrycan steadily over face, then chest, then thighs and then, bending the head now to the task, balanced the can on his right knee and poured carefully, using the left hand to wash his genitals.

He turned his head and smiled at me again. Then, in what I could only judge to be deliberate flirtation, instead of reaching for his robe first to cover his nakedness as any Tuareg man would have done, he rose to his feet, tensing the beautiful prominent haunches, and pulled on his incongruous dark-blue nylon Y-fronts, bought in the market-stalls of Nigeria. He rinsed his feet quickly and shoved them into his rubber sandals and then raised a hand and plucked a narrow reed flute from a bush where he had put it and came smiling to squat before me as I stood in the shelter of a little acacia.

"Why didn't you play the flute in Zaria, Kulutan?"

"You know, I had a flute before in Zaria but one day some boys were playing with it and it broke. I couldn't get another one of the kind I find pleasant." And he began to play a warbling mellow haunting tune in a minor key.

I ate him up with my eyes. The wonderful face, with strength and intelligence written all over it. Maybe I should have let the upper classes and their exclusiveness go hang and married him outright, causing a minor earthquake in terms of their society.

He paused. "Sit down," he said.

I sat with my back against the tree.

He played again, softly in a low gurgling key. His wet penis showed thick and soft and heavy through the thin nylon of the Y-fronts, the ridge of his circumcision clear. His eyes were downcast as he played and appeared not to see me staring.

He stopped abruptly. My eyes flew to his.

"I hear you frightened Hawa!" He was grinning broadly.

"Who's Hawa?"

"She's my cousin – the woman whose child you said was big."

I blushed. "*Kai*, I made a mistake. I didn't think what I was saying."

"It's nothing," he said lightly. "We told her you didn't mean any harm. That it is your people's custom to say things like that."

"True. Among us it's nothing." Not true. At home in Cork, wouldn't we always say "*She has a lovely head of hair, God bless her*" or "*He's a fine child, God bless him*"? The same as here – what I had forgotten was to say "by the grace of God" to avert any bad fortune. "I was just amazed that he was still drinking breast-milk."

"It's our habit," he said. "Me, my mother had *plenty* milk – she gave me breast-milk until I was very big. Until I could talk. Until I could run after her calling 'Wait, wait, *Ana*, I want to drink!'"

Why was it when any of them told me something in that tone of voice – as something really endearing or to be proud of – it invariably made me feel like slapping their faces? Why in God's name did I feel like that?

"I want to tell you something," he said abruptly.

"*To?*"

"I think I won't be able to go back with you to Zaria."

"How is that?" My voice was tight.

"You know, my master says that if I agree to stay and herd his animals for him he will give me a share. All his other Iklan are gone to Nigeria and Libya and he has nobody to work for him."

I felt a great dismay. It had never occurred to me that Kulutan would agree to stay. I had taken it for granted he would leave with us. My problem, I had thought, was to make sure that Sideka left too.

"Do you want to do that?" I asked. "To stay?"

"No."

"No? Well, he can't force you!"

"No – but he has no one – *surtout* if you take Sideka away now."

"Sideka? Tell me! Who is tending Aghali's animals now? Sideka is here with me, not minding goats! So who's minding the goats?"

"*Kai*, Aghali has to do it himself. But he is too old and you know his back is troubling him a lot."

"In the name of God! All your talk is nonsense! There are many boys around who can do it! Listen, listen to what I say: you – above all *you* – *must* come back! You can make a good life for yourself in Zaria. There's nothing here any more! You know there isn't!" Christ, even the bloody Sahara was advancing, to say nothing of the neighbouring countries and Niger itself squeezing the life out of pastoralist culture. I could tell him all this – he knew all this – but it would have no real effect.

"He won't agree." The shadow of thought had passed over his face like a grey tinge.

What was this? Was he, after all, unable to disobey his master?

Jesus. What was Aghali up to? It smacked of blackmail. But to which purpose? So that I would leave him Sideka? Or Kulutan? Whose freedom was it I would have to buy? Because I had no doubt that whatever way the wind blew it would end up with me forking out money.

"It's a pity you do not own a camel," he said.

What? To buy him with it? So that he could escape . . .

"I could cut its ear," he said.

"*What?*"

"I could cut its ear and belong to you." He was smiling faintly but there was a slight tenseness about his mouth and an intentness in his eyes that made it look as if he meant what he was saying.

"I don't understand. Its ear? Why?"

He grinned in pleasure when he realised I really didn't understand. He leant closer to me, so that our mouths were almost touching.

I dropped my gaze, only to be confronted with the sight of his penis stirring to erection inside the thin nylon underpants. I looked back up into his eyes, flushing.

"If I want to change masters," he said, holding my gaze, "all I have to do is cut off the ear of a camel belonging to the master I want."

"Just like that?"

"Only that."

What kind of fucking slavery was this? "Truly?"

"Truly. But you don't own a camel."

Maybe I could buy one.

"I will talk to Aghali," I said. I laid a hand on his knee.

The heat of his body radiated through his skin, holding my palm like a magnet. Our faces were still close. His lips moved. In a moment he would kiss me. He knew how. A certain market woman in Samaru who had taken a great fancy to him had taught him.

Hurriedly I pushed against his knee and rose clumsily. "Don't worry. I will talk with him."

The fierceness had gone out of the sun – soon it would begin to tint the sand rose-pink and the women would begin to pound the grain for the evening meal. As I sat with Ilyas and some of the men on a mat outside my tent, I saw a woman I didn't recognize approaching, leading a small boy by the hand. The little boy, some six years old, was naked and a thin stream of blood, half-dried, ran down his dusty leg from the tip of his penis. Dried tears streaked his dusty face. The woman was speaking vigorously with many gesticulations. I couldn't follow what she was saying. The boy stood impassively.

"Ilyas, what has happened?" I asked when I got a chance to interrupt.

"It is a dispute about some goats . . . "

"But the boy!"

"Ah! The *mallam* has just cut him. She wants you to give her some medicine."

A circumcision.

I crawled into the tent and, as I rummaged to see what I could find for him, I was surprised by feeling the now-familiar tide of anger and revulsion begin to rise. For some reason I didn't want to treat the little boy. I paused to try to define the feeling. Why? A thought surfaced. If they chose

to mutilate their child in this casual way let them deal with
it! Treating the wound was like drumming for the possessed
man – a collaboration.

I brushed the thought aside. I was uncertain what should
be done. Surely they had some traditional medicine?
Something that would be just as effective? But if I tried to
say that, they would hear it as a simple refusal. "Madame"
would be guilty of inexplicable Infidel meanness. What
should I do? Antiseptic and a bandage? Would a bandage
stick to the raw area? Should I wash the wound? Or would
that start the bleeding up again?

I went back outside, clutching my First Aid box, still
uncertain.

Sit him down somewhere clean. I sat him on an upturned
plastic washing-up basin and, squatting uncomfortably in
front of him, stared at his little penis. Jesus. What to do? His
mother was waiting impassively – there was always
something insolent in their asking – well, proud.

I had to wash it. But I was scared that might start the
bleeding again. "Did you wash him?" I asked the mother.

"Yes, indeed."

In the end I just applied the ointment thickly. He didn't
flinch though his thin little stomach contracted. Wasn't
circumcision usually a matter of great ritual? Weren't boys
circumcised in groups together? Yet here was this lone hero,
no drums beating, treated as casually as if he had cut his
finger or grazed a knee.

Now, to bandage or not to bandage? It would just get
filthy, wouldn't it? But still . . .

He was gazing at me solemnly. I smiled and was rewarded
with a wonderful gap-toothed grin.

So I had missed a circumcision. I should get a shot now at least. I squatted in front of him, staring at my sticky fingers, my mind racing. It seemed a heartless thing to do – to leap up and take a photograph. But . . . was I serious about keeping a record or not? I'd never make a professional photographer, that's for sure. If I put a bandage on his penis it would spoil the shot. The yellow basin was out, too. My yellow plastic basin was extraneous and atypical. To take a proper picture I would have to get up, wash my hands, stand the boy up next to his mother again, wash the ointment off too – hell, make him bleed again? What a grotesque idea . . .

"*Kai, Takafart!*" The mother was making a loose-limbed questioning gesture with her arm, palm upturned. The question was clear: have you finished? What the hell are you at?

I got up and washed my hands hastily, grabbed the camera and muttered something to Ilyas about taking a picture. He translated deadpan and the mother didn't react at all. I had no way of knowing whether they approved or not.

I quickly took a shot of the little creature on his plastic basin, gazing up at me wide-eyed, face streaked with dust and tears, little head with only a stubble of hair except for a cockscomb running along the top like a Sioux warrior, little penis glistening with antiseptic.

It was superb. But damn all good as a record of traditional culture.

*The Camera Always Lies.*

Isolated moments. Partial truths.

Then I took one shot with his mother standing next to him.

Enough. I felt like a criminal.

I unrolled a strip of gauze and wound it around his pathetic little penis, slinging the gauze around his narrow hips.

Later, everyone but Ilyas left and I seized the opportunity to ask him about Sideka's sex life.

"Tell me, Ilyas, has Sideka a girlfriend here? That he doesn't want to leave?"

He was stretched out at ease, arm beneath his head. He laughed. "Of course! But it's not serious, you know. Just play."

"What about yourself?"

He grinned slyly. "We all play, Ellen. But none of it is serious."

I wasn't getting very far.

"What about Haruna?"

A hoot of laughter, "I think Haruna has fucked every Iklan girl from here to Targa already and some of the others!"

While I goggled at this, wondering how much credence to give it, Amodi rode up on his camel, slid to the ground and came to join us. On to the next problem.

I waited with barely concealed impatience while he settled and relaxed and set up the tea things. And then I told them about Kulutan's dilemma. I badly needed their support, some light thrown on the question, some information on the inside track.

Amodi flipped the lid of the teapot closed and perched the pot on the pile of charcoal in the brazier. He stayed silent.

Ilyas, lounging on his side across from us, stayed silent too. There was an uneasiness in his silence. His eyes flickered from me to Amodi and back.

"What are we going to do?" I asked. "We have to help him."

Amodi brooded, eyes dark above his *tagilmoust*.

"Amodi?"

He gave a little sigh. "*To*, wait, let me tell you . . . "

The voice was too quiet. I knew this tone. It was what I called his false tone. This was Amodi about to deliver one of the great gobs of received prejudice he had grown up with. I knew him so well. He spoke, very quietly and carefully. "He must listen to what his master says."

I leapt to my feet in exasperation and walked off a few yards. I swung back. Stared at him, beside myself with frustration. He was better than that. He knew better than that. He *did*. I stared.

"*Kai*, woman," said Ilyas. "What has happened? Sit down, will you?"

There was a tension in Amodi's body, across his shoulders, but he wasn't looking at me. He was gravely contemplating his teapot.

He really was better than that. I knew him better than he knew himself. His good heart. His gentleness.

Calmly he arranged the tea glasses. Jesus, how I hated their calm!

"Bastard!" I hissed, to shatter it.

He looked at me in amazement.

Ilyas, startled, sat up.

"Kulutan doesn't want to stay! Why should he have to stay? There are many boys who can graze Aghali's goats!"

I started to walk away again.

"Ellen!"

I turned.

He had risen to his feet. He stopped to tuck the trailing end of his *tagilmoust* into the folds round his head. Then he stepped forward in his bare feet to confront me. "Listen – Kulutan's a slave! It is fitting that he does what Aghali says! My grandfather bought his grandfather in the slave market in Agadez and gave him to the grandfather of Aghali. He must do what Aghali says!"

The words fell like a judgment between us. A hot despair filled my heart. My life quaked like shifting sand beneath my feet. I was afraid and my fear tumbled me into blind rage. I raised a hand and struck him across the face – once, twice. He recovered in an instant and lunged for me but I twisted away, afraid now. He grabbed a short heavy piece of firewood and leapt forward. There was blood trickling from his nose.

He stood there facing me, the lump of wood raised in his hand.

I stood my ground.

Then, the wood dropped from his hand with a thud and he went down like a stone at my feet. His body extended itself and then began to jerk spasmodically – almost gently. I watched, terrified into immobility, as if my insides burned white with fear. He stopped with a long sighing groan and I saw the mucus streaming from his nostrils and urine stained his clothes. Then Ilyas was kneeling beside him, holding a little perfume bottle to his nose, and in a moment his eyes opened and he looked about in a dazed fashion.

I was frozen with shock and love and pity and guilt.

What was this? Epilepsy? Was he epileptic? Was that what the spirits he talked about were?

He had pinched his nostrils and was blowing the mucus onto the sand. I knelt beside him and used my scarf to wipe his face. He widened his eyes and closed his lips, pulling a face like a tired child and my heart went out to him. I felt the deepest shame at what I had reduced his bit of dignity to.

"It's his spirits," said Ilyas. "They have come back to him."

We took him into the tent and he lay down without a word, still dazed, and slept until the sun rose.

# Chapter 13

We dropped Ilyas and Kulutan back to Aghali's camp and left them there, Ilyas to spend time with his parents, Kulutan to settle the question of his return to Nigeria. I had wanted to talk to Aghali but Kulutan begged me to let him have another go.

When they arrived back by camel the very next day after sunset, it seemed to me a suspiciously fast return. Made me feel there was some agenda afoot that they were anxious to keep in motion.

I was glad that Amodi wasn't around when Kulutan indicated that I should walk out of the camp with him – Amodi was missing again. It seemed to me his disappearances were becoming more frequent and more prolonged. Kulutan and I sat down cross-legged, facing each other in the darkness. I felt very uneasy. This was a highly compromising situation. I wanted him to say what he had to say fast so we could get out of there.

"So, what happened with Aghali?" I asked.

"Madame, it's no use. I spoke to him again and I begged him. But he won't let me go." Kulutan's breath was coming a little fast. *Mister* Kulutan was losing his cool. "He still says if Sideka goes I must stay to herd the animals."

"In that case, take no notice of him! Just come!"

"I cannot." His insides of his thighs touched my crossed legs, almost in embrace.

"*Why* not?" I questioned savagely.

"*Kai*, I can't enter into a dispute with Aghali."

We were silent.

Then he said, "Sideka came to me and begged me to let him go."

Did I believe that? I had no idea. But I was sure that there was some bloody plot afoot.

I decided to take the plunge. "So what would happen if I gave Aghali money?"

"Money?"

"If I gave him money. Would he then be able to pay someone to herd his animals?"

"Maybe."

Yes, indeed. But would I be able to come up with enough money at this stage and still cover the trip back to Zaria?

We stayed like that, barely touching, for a while.

When he spoke at last his voice came caressingly, almost in a whisper. "Listen, madame . . . I have a secret to tell you . . ." A strong hand touched me lightly on the thigh.

I stared at him, waited, curious, not even afraid.

He hesitated, watching me. I should have known from the way he was watching me. The hand that had touched me withdrew. He watched me from under his eyelashes.

And still he hesitated.

"*To*. What is it?" I asked at last.

A few more moments and then he answered in a murmur. "Your *Amodi* . . . he is cheating you . . ."

*Oh God*. No. My mind froze in denial.

He gathered courage. "At night he is stealing himself away and visiting Lella, Sidi's daughter, over in the next camp."

The *Vogue* girl. His wife. Oh, God, to be flipped in a moment from health to pain.

"Do you know her?" he asked.

"His cousin?"

"No, no – she is not his cousin."

"A young girl? Beautiful – thin? Maryam told me she was his wife – that she was his first cousin."

"No – not her. That is Mona. No – Lella is her friend – they are always together. She is a beautiful girl. With a very fine body." The usual body movements that meant fat.

The girl at the well. The heavy girl. It was her. I knew.

He waited, watching my reaction.

I said nothing.

"Has he told you he will leave with you?" he asked abruptly.

"Yes." My voice sounded remote.

"He will not go," he said emphatically.

How to conceal the tumult in my heart? "*To*, we will see," I said.

"Do you know the gold ring you had made for him in Zaria? Ataka made it."

"Yes?"

"Amodi gave it to her. She is wearing it on her finger. I can show you."

One Tuareg ring looked much like another.

"He is leaving you at night and going to her tent," he whispered. "I can show you . . . I can take you to her sleeping place and you will see . . . ."

The thought filled me with terror.

"Do you want to?" he insisted.

I could not face such a thing.

"Have you seen them yourself with your own eyes?" I asked.

"Yes!"

That meant nothing. None of them knew the difference between a first-hand and a second-hand – or fifth-hand witness.

"Do you want to see them? To catch him?" he asked.

"No." I shook my head. This was a nightmare. I had to end it. "I'm very tired. I must go to sleep."

"*To*," he said, startled at my abruptness.

I got up at once. "Until tomorrow."

When I turned and looked back he was still squatting there, watching me go.


I sat in misery in the tent, thankful for the darkness that hid my tears from the women. I would have been glad for something cheerful to distract me until Amodi returned – from wherever he was. Instead Maryam chose that moment to announce casually, "We must begin to look for a husband for my Zainabu."

"Little Zainabu?" I said, pushing myself to make some feeble protest. "But she's only a little girl! How old is she? Eleven?"

"Twelve! She is nearly twelve!" put in Yassine.

"She's not old enough," I said, as calmly as I could.

"Not at all, not at all!" said Djanetta, who was sitting at the mouth of the tent, the dim light of a dusty moon playing on her. "Listen! The Prophet Muhammed, peace be on him – his youngest wife A'isha was only six years old when he married her!"

I froze. I was in no humour for this kind of conversation. I couldn't bear it at the best of times. I tried to think of something to distract Djanetta.

But Djanetta was away. "Listen! A certain *mallam* – a woman, told me this story – "

"The *mallam* who lives near here?" I interrupted but there was no heading her off.

"Indeed! Listen. She told me that when A'isha was thirteen years old the Prophet, peace be on him, took her with him to war."

I knew the bloody story already. So did all the others, no doubt, but nevertheless Djanetta had a captive audience. The older kids' mouths were dropping open in anticipation and she hadn't even started.

"She used to travel in a little house covered with a cloth on a camel. One night she left camp to urinate and her

161

necklace of shells fell from her neck and was lost in the sand. But she didn't notice that until she got back to camp. She went back to look for it – " She mimed A'isha's search in the sand with wide circles of her arms. "And while she was gone the men came to put her little house on the camel – you know, they were travelling at night – and they didn't know that she wasn't in the house because she was so young and had no weight. So they left and when A'isha came back they were gone. *To*, she covered herself in her wrapper and lay down in the sand – " She covered her face with her veil. "And a man called Safwan was passing on his camel – he had been left behind the rest of the army – and he saw her and dismounted. He said to her, 'Mount.' And she kept her face covered and she mounted and he took her back to the army. But the Prophet, peace be upon him, was very angry and all the people, even her parents, believed that Safwan had fucked her – " The fucking symbol of a finger through a closed fist. "His son-in-law Ali told him, 'Women are many. Divorce her. Just change her.' But the Prophet Muhammed, peace be on him, was very worried. *Very!* He fell into a trance and they left him there with a leather pillow under his head – " The head on the pillow was mimed with her folded hands. "And he heard the voice of Allah speaking to him and telling him that A'isha had no fault. So he sat up and the sweat was falling from him – " She shook her arms as if scattering drops of sweat. "And because of that he said that it was necessary that four people should be witnesses before anyone was accused of adultery. And also Allah told him that no one was allowed to talk to or see his wives and that they must keep their faces covered – " She covered her face, her two hands forming a yashmak across her nose and mouth. "And therefore," she paused and finished with triumphant satisfaction, "that is why you see the Arab women with their faces covered."

Happy ending indeed. Lucky for Muhammed that Allah decided to speak up. He might have lost his child-bride.

And that, I thought, in a nutshell, is the difference between Islam and Christianity. The thought of the austere altruistic Jesus falling into a trance to justify his marriage to a child . . . or telling his disciples that it was OK for them to use *azl* – coitus interruptus – on a bunch of captured women, though full rape was out because it was already arranged that the women should be ransomed. Or what of the time Allah again came to his rescue when he found himself lusting unlawfully after Zainab, the wife of his adopted son? Muhammed fell into a trance and Allah said that it was His Will that Muhammed should marry the girl which Muhammed piously hastened to do, waking up and saying "Who will go to Zainab and tell her the good news, that Allah has married her to me?" I just hoped Zainab didn't care for her husband.

*Blessed are the clean of heart . . .*
*Blessed are the merciful . . .*
*Blessed are the peacemakers . . .*
*Blessed are those who hunger and thirst after justice . . .*
Trances. They certainly had precedents for trances.

"In that case, why don't you Tamajegh women cover your faces, Djanetta? You are Muslims."

"It is not our habit."

I passed a tent where the women were working on repairs to
a goatskin tent they had spread across their laps. Right in
the opening, on the left-hand side was Lella, the girl Amodi
was supposed to be sleeping with. She turned her head and
looked at me serenely, sitting cross-legged on her generous
haunches, black wrapper pulled tight on her thighs, a trace
of a smile on her rounded gorgeous face.

I took a picture.

*Oh, the eyebrows and white teeth of my beloved!*
*Her hair glistens with yellow butter and mirrors the sun and*
*the moon,*
*Her eyes are as round as a ring in the water*
*When it has been cleft by a stone.*
*Last night I spent in sadness and despair*
*For she whom I love and who has set my soul on fire was far*
*away,*
*My heart is cut in two within my breast*
*And when my soul beholds her image*
*My liver is on fire.*
*Tears run down my cheeks and my eyes will not stop weeping.*
*Oh you unhappy eyes, how will you find peace?*

*Dinbidin is making herself beautiful today, like a panther*
*Under the Deg'elet and Afarfar tree.*
*She does not eat, she does not work, and none can match her.*

*She is better than dates, better than millet, and cheese put
together.*
*Better than the shady Tereket tree in the sandy plain.*
*Fetch more wood for the fire,*
*Clap your hands,*
*It is good to celebrate!*
*Soon you too will be dead!*
*How many there are for whom no more wedding tents are
built!*

Did I believe it? I didn't know what to believe. But I was in
a fever of tension now, tormented with jealous images. I felt
a kind of horror. Whenever I was alone, I made myself dwell
on images of Amodi's hands on that curving flesh, Amodi's
nose pressed against hers drawing in her breath, his lips
whispering phrases in Tamajegh in her ear, his hands
caressing her rounded breasts, undoing her soft black
wrapper, plunging between those generous thighs – what
then? What would she allow? Would she? Would she?
Would she let him? If she wanted him, if she wanted him to
stay, if she wanted to keep him from me, yes, she would.
Why not? Pregnancy? That would be her winning card. And
what risk? He – or indeed any of the others – would marry
her at least for the duration of the pregnancy, to save the
child from stigma. They were are all the same family – the
child would look like one man as much as the next. Where
was the problem? Of course this must happen all the time.

A small cold voice in my head said, *What an excellent system*. And I thought with a kind of savage admiration, *Trust them to come up with something so simple and humane . . .*

"You know, Ellen," said Haruna that night, in his nice Cork accent, "these girls – they have really good asses for fucking. They are so soft and they stick out. It feels really good."

Surely not? Surely they wouldn't let Haruna?

"Haruna . . . do you think that's really true about Amodi and that girl?" Kulutan had told Ilyas and Ilyas had told Sideka and Sideka had told Haruna.

He was silent, eyes cast down. The generous lips closed over his prominent teeth, his teeth like an elephant. "I think . . . you have given Amodi all your heart . . . but he has given you only part of his."

That said it all.

I walked off into the silence alone and there, alone, I knelt and beat my head on the sand, beating the images out.

And cried but with some restraint. No one must hear me.

I needed to howl.

I stumbled to my feet and set blindly off until I began to be afraid of getting lost though I could still hear the distant bleating of goats.

I stopped and listened. Nothing but the faintest of distant cries, animal and human.

I knelt again and at first with some awkwardness and feeling of dry falsity I summoned up my images of him with her and raised my voice and cried and lowered my head and beat it on the sand, hurting myself. Then I felt it gather force and possess me like madness and I howled in anger and grief and pain.

I thrashed on the sand sobbing.

And then I listened and grew nervous and felt sure that someone must be lurking, if only Haruna or Ilyas or Sideka. Was that a giggle? There was no one.

I could feel eyes on me.

There was a faint sound again, like a woman's voice faintly chattering.

It was a night of *harmattan* dust and not clear. I couldn't see very far.

I knew there was no one there.

But I was now sober and fearful.

The dreadful embarrassment . . . if anyone saw . . .

I rose shakily and pulled my clothes straight, watching. There was no one.

Ears straining, I began to move towards the faint distant bleats and cries.

Suddenly something loomed up in front of me. I swore and, heart hammering, circled around a large mound covered with dry branches. It was a burial place, Amodi had told me, a place of the spirits – the *Kel Ténéré* – the "people of the empty places". A place to be feared.

I hurried towards the human voices.

# Chapter 14

Ilyas and I were going to the well. We had been sitting with Djanetta while she conducted a desultory lice-hunt in Ilyas's head – more for the comfort-value of a bit of friendly grooming than anything else.

"Where's Zainabu? I told her we were going and that we would take her. Isn't she coming?" I asked Ilyas, as I slung my camera over my shoulder.

"No, she's drinking milk," he answered, pulling on his sandals.

"Well, until we wait for her? Or is it not so?"

"No, no, she won't have got her ease."

"Ease? What is your meaning?" I was puzzled.

"After drinking milk her stomach will be swollen," Djanetta put in. "She will feel pain for a while. Just go and leave her."

"Is she not well? I saw her just now – she was fine."

"No, no – she's just drinking milk." She made to rise and then paused, seeing my face. "Don't you understand?" she asked uncertainly.

I shook my head. "No . . . "

"*To!*" she exclaimed with an air of excitement.

Suddenly she caught me by the wrist and pulled me out of the tent. I just managed to protect the camera with my forearm as it swung against the tent-pole.

"Come! Come!" she said excitedly and conspiratorially, gesturing to a neighbouring tent. She caught at my wrist again and drew me with her to the tent and then ducked under the low-hanging skin. I followed using my usual awkward embarrassing squat.

A chorus of voices greeted me.

I noticed Chimbizat, Kulutan's Akli friend, lying on a mat opposite. He was the only man present. "Madame!" he cried warmly, raising a friendly hand.

I was given a place to sit on a bed next to an old woman who began to fondle me, tucking loose-flying strands of my hair into my plaits, stroking my arms. A glass of hot tea was pressed into my hand. I drank it off. It was the nauseatingly sweet third glass.

"Look! Look! Ellen!" Djanetta was pulling at my arm.

I looked.

On the sand on the other side of the bed little Zainabu
lay on her back, knees raised and spread apart, wearing only
her black wrapper. Mouth open. An index finger was
hooked into each corner of her mouth, spreading her lips in
a grotesque grin.

"Ellen!" called Maryam who sat on the sand beside her, a
kettle poised in her hand. "Djanetta says you have never
seen this. Look now!" She tilted the kettle and a steady
stream of milk began to pour into the wide slit made by the
girl's stretched mouth.

"You see, Ellen?" asked Djanetta eagerly. "Until she
becomes a beautiful woman!"

The hot surge of rage was instantaneous. The sweat
sprang out in my palms and the nerves in my face began
to jump. Oh, God, I thought, I mustn't. I must keep
control.

The milk continued to pour, inexorable. Zainabu retched
but managed to control it, choking down the milk. Her
mouth closed and Maryam righted the kettle, cutting off the
stream.

"Well, God punish you, open your mouth!" her mother
cried. "By the Will of God, I don't know what to do with
her! Yesterday she vomited half her milk and today she
wants to do the same! Open your mouth, wretch!"

Zainabu pulled her lips back again but began to whimper.
The white stream began to pour again.

What was happening? My brain fumbled among my half-
baked bits of science. It must be a way to get the milk into
her stomach but by-passing some stage of digestion in the
mouth – so that the sugar – the fat – would not be broken
down . . . in any case to make it more fattening. Or was it

simply to do with the mechanics of the thing – a way to pack more in?

Zainabu was choking again. Tears slid from the corners of her slanted eyes.

Maryam paused again and waved her kettle at me. "Look at her, Ellen! She has no body at all yet she refuses to drink! If you saw the girls in the camp over beyond the well! Such fine bodies they walk with difficulty!"

"Old Mushashi really knows how to force them!" said Djanetta. She turned to me. "You know, until one of her granddaughters died because of drinking milk last year."

"Never, never!" came the gravelly voice of the old woman beside me. "That was not her granddaughter. That was a girl from another family that she was forcing."

"She died?" I fought to control my voice. "How is that?"

"Yes, yes," said Maryam. "It's true that sometimes girls die."

"Their hearts stop," said Djanetta as if she were imparting some juicy bit of gossip.

"But there's no fear of that with this little wretch here!" cried Maryam and she slapped her daughter vigorously on the head – once, twice – and Zainabu dragged her lips into a wide grimace again. Maryam poured.

"Open your legs!"

Why the legs? It was degrading, some obscene parody of the sexual act – my skin crawled at it and the pit of my belly tightened as if I were witnessing a pornographic act.

The kettle was empty. Maryam lifted a mat covering a large wooden bowl and filled the kettle again while Zainabu gagged and struggled to control herself. Her mother slapped the side of her head and raised the kettle again.

Zainabu began to whimper helplessly and I started as Chimbizat suddenly leapt to his feet. In a mock rage, he stood astride the girl and, pulling a leather whip from his sword-belt, brandished it threateningly over her.

"Before God, I'll beat you until your skin comes off if you don't open your throat!"

Anger burst like a hot liquid inside me. My hand shot out and I slammed the kettle to the ground.

I heard Maryam cry out. "The milk is gone! My daughter will die for lack of it!"

I stumbled out of the tent and kept going. Through the circle of withered trees and scrub and on across the sand. My camera hung heavily, a useless weight. I stopped and held it in my hands, glaring at it as if it were the focus of my anger. My hands were trembling.

I went and sat in a hollow behind a ridge of sand near a little acacia tree and tried to quiet myself. The tears came now, as they always did when the anger had vented itself.

Then, at last, head on knees, I listened to the silence that was not really silence: the distant cries from the camp, the lowing of animals, the steady beat of wooden pestle on mortar, the indefinable sound of air moving among the dry grasses. The peace of the empty spaces was deep and tangible. How to relate this healing silence to the obscene thing I had just witnessed? Jesus, who had first conceived such an obscene notion? Like foot-binding or genital excision – it had to have started somewhere, in someone's brain. Who? When? Man or woman? Whether man or woman, here as usual were the women cheerfully and with gusto embracing the tradition, with ferocity turning everything into a weapon against themselves.

It made me want to lie down and die.

I remembered – I had heard that the Arabs go one better and use little instruments of torture like wooden toe-screws to help the process along. Chimbizat's stagey threats were nothing to that.

*No pain, No gain.*

When I sighed it tore through my chest.

*She is dazzling harmony:*

*A full, shining moon,*

*Scarred with stretch-marks are her belly and flanks –*

*Vast expanses of exquisite softness . . .*

My thoughts shifted. What a fool I was! What had I accomplished? Nothing. They would have no idea what my anger signified.

I stared at the camera. I had let the picture of a lifetime go down the drain in a torrent of useless emotion. That would have been of some value, some use. I had to get a grip. I could only be a witness to this beautiful and bitter experience. But to be a good witness I had to become detached.

Dust stood thick in the near distance. The *harmattan* was now here with a vengeance, veiling and obscuring everything. It was cold. The rainy season with its celebrations and abundance seemed a bright pulsing phantom. The gleam of leaves, the phosphorescent whites and blues of clothing, the gleam of golden skin and purple metallic glint of indigo, laughing faces dipped in huge wooden bowls of frothing milk – all against a silver sand and brilliant sky – the pulsing excitement of the racing drumbeat, a clear flooding moon, voices soaring in vigorous song, white camels dramatic in red and green blankets, leather fringes fluttering, dark eyes

gleaming, silver crosses and golden necklaces sparkling in
sunlight, the great pulsing affirmation of Tuareg life – a huge
greedy cry of "Yes!" bounding to the endless sky . . .

All eclipsed by this red dust, all dulled, patina eroded.

Hunger. Would the grain last? Would the animals
survive? Would the men ever return? From Nigeria? From
Libya?

Would we be allowed to live?

Amodi was approaching across the sand, his white open-
sided robe billowing.

God damn it! Was he going to be all-wise, all-forgiving
again?

What was he carrying? A baby?

He sat cross-legged in front of me without a word,
cradling in his arms a little gazelle, a tiny delicate little
jumble of limbs with two great dark eyes that stared at me.

"Ah!" I sighed and I stroked its head. The little animal
seemed to have no fear. Or else was too weak to react.

I loved the way he was holding it so gently.

I loved him.

And my period hadn't come, not yet.

"It's yours," he said.

"What! Where did you get it?"

"Its mother was killed. Abu Bakr gave it to me for you.
To take back to Zaria."

My heart quailed. This was a baby.

"But . . . it will die . . . "

"No, people rear them. It won't die."

I took the beautiful frail little creature, eyes like Ataka's,
and I was full of misgivings.

It was an omen. And I was afraid.

"Don't worry," he said. "They think you were just upset about Zainabu."

I looked at him. And what do *you* think? What do you think I was upset about? Or do you mean they can't be expected to understand a *Takafart's* inexplicable temper?

"Why are they doing that stupid thing?" I asked.

"Ah, Ellen," he said gently. "You saw Zainabu last year when she was small and thin. See how she is now, how fine her body is! Which one is better?"

"I preferred her last year," I said and I, rather than he, seemed pettish and silly.

He said nothing, just cast his eyes down in his serene way.

I could never bear to hurt him. My feelings for him were tender, sometimes more like a mother's for a child. Couldn't bear to let him be hurt. I loved him.

I leant forward and kissed him, proffering the only thing that could cross all barriers and differences.

We sat for a long time, holding the gazelle together, kissing, leaning our foreheads together.

I had to say it and I said it trembling. "When will we leave?"

"We'll leave the day after tomorrow."

The relief that flooded through me was a warm and heady flood, like champagne. I was weak with it.

He flicked his robe back over his shoulder and I watched him push the great soapstone bracelet down his arm, freeing the cluster of leather charms about his sword-arm. He pulled them off and took one from the bunch: a little dark-red tooled leather rectangle, almost black with sweat. I thought he was about to give it to me or, for an incredulous moment,

175

that he was about to put it on the little gazelle – if anyone would do such a thing, he would. But he rose to his feet and walked to the nearby acacia. Wondering, I watched him reach high and tie the charm by its black string to a branch of the tree. He stood back and murmured what seemed to be a prayer, then looked once more in quiet satisfaction and came back to me. Smiling, he pulled me to my feet. I pushed his robe aside so I could lean against the warmth of his bare chest, the gazelle between us.

The gazelle and our child? My belly throbbed at the thought.

"Why have you tied the charm?" I asked then, my face against his skin.

"It will call to us after we leave this place so we will always come safely back." I felt his smile against the top of my head.

When we walked back to camp Zainabou was still weeping, sitting in the sand, wrapper loosened, legs stretched out, belly distended.

# Chapter 15

The men were muttering again in the way that made me uneasy. I boldly joined them, sitting on one of the mats. It was war-talk again.

It probably always was. I had been crazy to think it was about Amodi.

I listened but caught little. This time they definitely didn't want me there. Talk descended into guttural mutterings behind *tagilmousts* with the occasional "How are you, madame?" thrown my way out of courtesy. I wondered how soon I could get up and leave them without losing too much face. I racked my brain for a pretext as I listened, head lowered.

There were meaningful and guarded references to Tchin Tabaraden, to the police there – and oddly numerous mentions of "young men".

I began to surmise that someone – some young men – were in conflict with the police, perhaps in Tchin Tabaraden.

My heartbeat quickened.

Then a mention of guns.

Christ.

Who?

Some young fools – or some poor innocents?

I didn't want to hear. And I hated the avid way they talked of these things like idiots or children.

*Bang, Bang, You're dead.*

They hadn't a fucking clue. They were always high in a cloud-cuckoo land where they could all drive Landrovers without lessons and massacre a dozen policemen before breakfast without guns. The dream world was strong in them. Too strong. Like children.

*I'm going to be an astronaut when I grow up.*

*I'm going to be World Heavyweight Champion Boxer.*

*I'm going to be a millionaire.*

*I'm going to be a famous rock star.*

*I'm going to be Lawrence of Arabia and live with nomads in the desert.*

I got up at last, awkwardly, and strolled off as casually as I could.

Amodi was missing again.

That evening just before sundown, as the men lined up to pray, Ilyas and I saddled up my camel and, with me in the saddle and him astride the back of the hump, we went for a wild prolonged gallop. At least it felt like a wild prolonged gallop to me – to any Tuareg it probably looked like a tentative prologue to a wild gallop. The fall of darkness brought a halt to our ride. We headed back to camp at a walking pace. We had just dismounted when we heard them.

"*Ellen! Ellen!*"

"Ellen!"

Yassine and Djanetta were gesturing in great excitement.

"Ellen, Muroniya has come! We will have an *ahal* tonight!"

"We will drink sweetness!"

Their excitement knew no bounds and my own heart lifted.

"Good! That's good," I said with pleasure. "But . . . "

"Come, come!" They left off gesturing and grabbed me, one on each side, and pulled me onwards.

"Hey! Where are you pulling me? Wait!" I resisted a little, leaning back, laughing at their enthusiasm. "An *ahal* – isn't that only for unmarried people?"

"Yes, yes – it's not exactly an *ahal* – just a celebration! Come, come, come!" They gestured and pulled and I went with them.

They dragged me to Maryam's tent. I had never made an easier or more rapid entrance – they practically scooped me off the ground between them in their zeal.

Inside, I was confronted by Tuareg womanhood in all its glory.

An enormous woman sat on Maryam's bed, glittering and gleaming with gold and silver and burnished indigo. Her rounded face was decorated with delicate patterns in red and black; a yellow line was drawn from forehead down the bridge of her nose. A cluster of Agadez crosses strung on leather cords around her neck lay over several necklaces of long golden beads. The great curving circles of heavy silver hung from her elongated earlobes – or rather, while one did, the other was looped back up and around the ear. Blue glass and silver bracelets clustered on her wrists; her great haunches were swathed in blue-black cloth with a satin sheen; the white lace shirt that fell over her great breasts was criss-crossed with the red embroidered lattice-work typical of Agadez, rather than the Tchin Tabaraden type with its gracefully designed square yoke embroidered in black. On her head she wore a great turban of purple burnished indigo. A wealth of glossy plaits swung around her face.

They pushed me forward and she smilingly greeted me as if I were a supplicant before a queen, treating me to the stroking repetitive handshake, while I muttered the responses to her greetings in some embarrassment, and eventually raising me to sit beside her on the bed.

"What's her name? What's her name?" she was saying. No embarrassment for her. She was a princess.

"El-len."

"El-len! My friend!" She stared in some fascination at my jeans and then began to stroke my thighs with her fingers. "Look, she's wearing trousers. But she's shy! Look!" She was stroking me down, fondling my hand as if we were lifelong friends.

I smiled and smiled and smiled.

They gave her tea but she pressed it on me, the bitter first cup. I drank it off while they handed her another.

"Look, Ellen!" Djanetta was holding out an *imzad* to me, a narrow lute-like instrument with just a single string. I then realised that this was the Muroniya from Tillia, the famous beauty and *imzad*-player.

"And we are bringing the drum from the other camp!"

Ah, the drum. The *ettebel*.

And the spirits in its wake.

I vowed that this time I would be there with my camera. This time I would catch those spirits on film like the protoplasm blobs of early mediumship.

And photograph I did. Shamelessly. As if by doing so I was atoning for all the wallowing in wasteful emotion that had been thrust upon me. This was some form of vindication at last.

The decorated camel-bags were unslung from the tent-poles and the dust was slapped from their surfaces. All the hidden finery was pulled out and laid out, the remnants of an affluent past, still hoarded and treasured. The dusty black cloth was cast aside and hips were swathed in shiny satin, bare breasts were covered with lacy white embroidered shirts, lengths of *ilesham* were draped over heads or swirled about them.

I photographed the face-painting which was done with a gleeful solemnity, faces alive peering into little scraps of hand-mirror.

And of course I too had to be painted and swathed and turbaned.

I gave little Muhane a white scarf to twist around her head and Yassine supplied a length of blue lace to drape over her shoulders. With a black line running down her nose and yellow and red markings on her cheeks, making her look like a Hallowe'en cat, she was proud and beaming as she posed for her picture.

And, with the gathering clogging *harmattan*, it really was something like Hallowe'en, the autumn festival before the bleak of winter, a last chance to wallow in a little abundance before dust and hunger came down like a pall.

News of Muroniya's presence must have spread like wildfire through the dry scrub or perhaps the insistent drumbeat driven by the women was audible to keen desert ears from a great distance. I suddenly had an image of the news being passed from drum-group to drum-group like Indian smoke-signals. At any rate, camels began to appear and kept coming as the evening drew on.

But again no Amodi. I kept expecting to wheel about, camera poised, to find him in my sights wearing his precious *ilesham*, the one we had bought together in Kano, with great silver decorations attached.

But he didn't come. The questions I dared to ask met with vague responses. An undercurrent of tension moved along my bloodstream like the fever of the drumbeat itself.

The great Muroniya was holding court in the traditional manner, her tent crammed with joking flirting men, young women ranged round like her handmaids assisting her in keeping up the banter. She wasn't so young, herself, but that didn't seem to bother anyone. In the early hours the suitors would disperse, some of them already knowing by the tweak of a toe or pinch of the calf that a particular woman wanted him to sneak back later for surreptitious lovemaking. Others, including the lucky man who would make love to Muroniya, would say goodbye with the traditional stroking handshake, waiting for the pressure of a finger or the flick of a fingernail digging into the palm which would be the signal that said, "I want you". It was amazing: a culture based on worship of women.

Nobody minded me taking the pictures, in fact they preened and posed. I snapped away happily, for once too intent on what I was doing to be embarrassed at my awkwardness as I squatted with aching muscles under the hang of the tent-leather, balancing on the pads of my feet instead of firmly on the flat of the feet as they did. The crisp new cloth with its purple satin sheen that they had wrapped around me bunched awkwardly around my waist, the newness of the material making it difficult to tuck in securely. I kept almost losing it as I twisted to get photo angles and I knocked the turban over my eyes so often that I eventually pulled it off and hung the length of it around my neck where it then constantly got in the way of the camera.

The men had started to sing sporadically, beginning in ragged disorganised feints that eventually burst into the brisk vigorous pace that always put me in mind of a trotting camel barely held in check; the rhythmic clapping and the counterpointing voices excited me – reminding me of a childhood of following pipe bands, the skirling of the bagpipe setting up a fever in my blood that made me want to follow the kilted pipers to the ends of the earth if needs be. But they always eventually stopped beside some lorry or bus on the outskirts of town or city centre and with a desultory few final rolls of the drum or notes of the pipes it would be over. And I would have to turn and go home. When the driving wild rhythms of the Tuareg singing petered out in the same casual way, the singer lapsing into chat, I nearly shook the singers in frustration – *More! More! More! Don't stop!* It was never ever enough.

The lads were sitting at the tent opening, almost squeezed out into the dark on this occasion. Sideka was smiling seductively over at me as he "danced" sitting in place, head, neck and body rhythmically keeping time in a riding-a-camel motion, hand making the "camel" imitation – raised to eye level, flat and rigid with the thumb raised – like in the game of throwing animal shadows on the wall. This was the standard style of getting into the music – the arm and hand made the rhythmic camel movement, the body and head followed suit and the face invariably assumed that special smiling seductive expression. As the whole tent surged to the rhythms, I pushed my way over to the lads. Haruna was clowning as usual. *"Move yourself, woman!"* he cried, slapping at my shoulder with the palm of his hand in the approved way, almost knocking me over from my insecure perching squat.

I righted myself and scrambled out tripping over wrapper and turban, the weight of the swinging camera almost throwing me off balance again.

A strong arm pulled me safely to my feet. Kulutan.

*"Ikon Allah!* The Will of God!" he said, laughing softly. "Is our madame trying to kill herself here in Niger?"

He was dressed in his traditional best, wearing his

*tagilmoust.* I actually preferred him wearing his Hausa embroidered pill-box hat.

"Kulutan! How goes it?"

"All is peace."

The singing behind me was winding down erratically to one of its pauses. Then suddenly a hush fell.

"Have you seen Amodi?" I asked quietly but as casually as I could, fearing I could be overheard.

"No," he said.

But I didn't know whether to believe him. A thought struck me. Where was Lella? While I tried to phrase the question he started, raising a finger.

Muroniya had begun to play the *imzad*. The anguished notes of the one-stringed lute, played with a little bow, vibrated in the air . . . and here was the real Tuareg passion . . .

*Humbly I honour the deeds of Allah,*
*He has given to the imzad –*
*The one that has an eye that isn't living –*
*A power far nobler than a soul.*
*Now it has begun to play all is silent;*
*Men fall dumb, only stirring a hand*
*To pull the turban over their eyes.*
*Thanks to your imzad, O daughter of Ekli,*
*Allah has given me back my life.*

We knelt again in the tent entrance and he put an arm around me. Then he dropped it as movement behind told us that people were spilling out of the other tents, dragging mats and sitting themselves down.

"Come outside!" shouted Kulutan. "Muroniya! Come out where we can see you! Your people are sitting here outside!"

She heard him and paused. Yes, she would come.

I searched the crowd behind me for Amodi. For Lella.

Kulutan was pulling me back. We gave place to Muroniya as they helped her to a mat at the tent entrance. The tent behind her emptied.

She raised the little bow and a hush fell again.

This almost harshly haunting music was more of an acquired taste. It didn't slide as easily into my blood as the drumbeat, the flute or the voices.

But it held them enthralled.

I itched to photograph the rapt faces. Then it struck me that I could possibly use the zoom lens – the flash would still disturb but if I were at a distance . . .

I hesitated, afraid to take the plunge, afraid my movement would be the stone in the water that would break the absorption. Only just in time I bethought myself: I couldn't move – it would appear to be an insult to Muroniya's art. I was stuck. For once I had to absorb the rapture, the beauty of the faces, with my mind's eye and no camera lens.

But later when they built a huge fire I managed to get some pictures. Muroniya continued to play and the firelight fluttered on faces on which the *imzad* depicted all the anguish and rapture of desert life. I saw tears roll down the weathered cheeks of some of the older men.

Their cultural emblems: the camel, a noblewoman playing the *imzad*.

And what of the other? The raised sword? Did I even believe in that?

There was dust over the moon which no longer rode clear. It had become cold.

I wrapped the opened turban around me like a shawl and considered going back to my tent to get a sweater. Yet tonight, it would be odd to the point of discourteous to huddle in a sweater when everyone else was in their lace and light cotton.

Amodi had not appeared. Nor could I see Lella.

I laid my head on my raised knees and hugged my misery.

And then a new rhythm started up. A group of young girls, probably Inaden, had lined up in a swaying bending row and begun "Sharibu" to a brisk handclap . . .

*I want Sharibou,*
*For years I've wanted him*
*And until the world is destroyed I'll want him!*
*I want Sharibou,*
*My heart is sick but because of him*
*It manages to carry a great load.*
*I can't talk of anything but Sharibou*
*My heart has a path for Sharibou in it.*
*Sharibou collects tax among the people,*
*He has great learning,*
*His tagilmoust is like a well-rope because it is so long,*
*His leather bag is covered in fringes.*
*He went to a well where there were many people with their animals,*
*Sharibou took water before anyone else for his animals and went off!*
*He sits on a fine mat,*
*He has a fine blanket for his camel,*
*His camels are white and black . . .*

And with the close of the Inaden song, the drumbeat resonated. Two women were sitting one a side, the flats of their palms beating the *ettebel* – *raa-tat-tat-tat*-tat, *raa-tat-tat-tat*-tat – a powerful rhythm that only a lifetime of pounding millet had given them the muscle power to produce. They sent it out into the night without let or pause.

A handclap started up again and a wild sky-lifting cry shot to the stars.

"*Hey, Ellen!*" called Ilyas laughingly from across the circle of the fire, making the pushing motion with his palm towards me even though he couldn't touch me.

I laughed and returned the gesture.

Where was Amodi?

I laughed.

We clapped and sang until most of the men were on their feet in a shuffling stamping dance punctuated by piercing war-cries and the women began to ululate shrilly, a sound to make the blood fly to the sky. I stood too and went to where my lads stood clapping in wild excitement and clapped with them, giving myself to the rhythm. The drumbeat sped on.

Two others had replaced the women on the drum.

When the first figure fell I felt a faint sense of shock, but it was muted as if I had been waiting for it. It was a man and he rolled himself into a frenzy on the sand, the others stepping out of his way but otherwise ignoring him.

We clapped and danced on. My heart quickened and my breath came short.

A cry arose from where the women were sitting and I glanced over to see a small woman – could it be Yassine? – on her feet, her body jerking spasmodically.

On into the night we went and I was still there when Ilyas fell thrashing about at my feet.

I clapped on. *Let him*.

And then I felt it, the familiar crawling sense of disgust and revulsion. And yet I clapped, camera still jerking on its strap against my ribs. This time the spirits would not expel me from their territory. Yes, that was what had happened before – suddenly it seemed clear with the clarity of intoxication. Simply that. They didn't want me there. I was a foreigner. I had no place.

But this time I would not go.

I was drunk on rhythm and almost no longer felt my body. My hands were numb as they beat together, and I no longer consciously controlled them. They seemed to clap of their own volition, riveted to the clapping hands of Sideka next to me – his hands were moving mine, puppet-like.

I saw the same tranced high-stepping dance before me, the dance I had first seen Amodi's uncle do that night they came.

Somewhere, but removed, my brain was working. Thinking: they all react in individual ways to the spirits, there is no one reaction.

I saw Ataka tearing past me wildly, his face a staring mask. Some others pursued him.

I no longer felt my body. And suddenly I was above it, looking down at how it worked so hard at its clapping and rhythm.

I saw Ataka's friends stop him as he headed into the dusty murkiness of the desert. I saw them lead him back, his face blank like a man awaking and bemused.

And yet I was still in my body because now I felt a strange and unpleasant tugging at my heels. As if a magnetic force in the earth had grasped my feet and now would make me dance puppet-like. My feet were making a short stepping motion, perhaps no more than a shuffle but it felt to me as if I were taking giant steps, raising the feet as high as the man with his high-stepping dance and slamming back down to earth again like the giant in *Jack and the Beanstalk*.

Each step like the pulling up of roots.

I pulled against it, wrenching my feet against it.

And then suddenly, like an elastic band snapping, it was gone.

It had let me go. It didn't want me.

Kulutan's face was before me. Grave. A bit calculating.

My body was drenched in sweat. I shivered in the cold. His hands were on my shoulders and I could feel them.

The drumbeat was fading. We were walking away from it. I was walking away and I was cold and conscious.

We went so far I couldn't hear the drum any more.

He halted me and pulled me down to sit. "What happened to you just now?" he asked.

I couldn't answer.

"The spirits caught you," he said.

I shook my head.

I think we sat for a long time.

I saw the swaying lights of the Land Cruiser before I even heard the quiet purr and occasional revving of the engine.

Then I realised he had heard it long before me.

"Your boy has come looking for us," he said.

I knew he meant Haruna but I thought of Amodi. It must be Amodi, returned.

The headlights were blindingly upon us.

It was Haruna with Ilyas. "What brought you here?" I asked in some irritation when they got out.

Ilyas was carrying the little gazelle which I had privately named Zincad – simply the Tamajegh word for gazelle.

"*Kai*, woman, we thought you were lost or the spirits had run away with you!" said Ilyas. "We didn't even know Kulutan was with you." He looked askance at Kulutan.

Jesus. How did this look? Me and Kulutan in traditional *tête à tête* on a night of courtship?

Haruna was glowering too.

"I saw she was not well," said Kulutan, "so I followed her."

They sat. Ilyas with supple Tuareg limbs that folded comfortably every which way, Haruna with raised knees, his heavier muscular legs looking awkward in comparison.

"Has Amodi come back?" I asked nervously.

"No," said Ilyas, "we haven't seen him."

This was crazy! Where the hell was he?

"I know where he is," said Kulutan almost slyly.

"Where?" I asked bluntly.

He stayed silent for a while, staring at the sand.

"*Where?*" I asked again, my heart thumping.

He raised his head and still hesitated, biting his lip.

Then, seeing my glare, he answered.

"Out there," he said, with a sweep of his hand towards the murkiness about us.

*What?*

Haruna looked bemused but light seemed to be dawning on Ilyas.

"Where?"

"He is with Lella," said Kulutan. "They are together out there."

"In another camp?"

"No – in the desert – alone."

"How do you know?"

"Two of the Iklan boys saw them when they were walking from another camp. Behind a small hill out there."

A sort of horror crept over me.

They were arguing about it.

"I can show you," said Kulutan. "We can find them."

"*To*," said Haruna decisively, clambering to his feet. "Let's go." He jiggled the car-keys in his hand.

"In the *car*?" I asked.

"Yes," he said. "That way we will get them quickly. I'm not spending the night trekking through this bloody bush."

It was madness. But I was mad. I must have been mad to find myself with the others tensely seated in the Land Cruiser, swaying through the darkness.

Haruna revved enough in the deep sand to frighten off a platoon of lovers.

It was terrifying – the noise of the engine filling our universe, the headlights distorting our vision, fear of finding him, fear of failing. We persisted, caught in the madness of the hunt, the desire to chase a creature to death, wending our way recklessly around mounds and sparse bushes and hillocks with the powerful beam of the headlights washing over the landscape, picking out strange shapes and movements and deceptive shadows. Once we stopped and I sweated it out while Kulutan and Haruna went to confront what we took to be a couple of lovers but turned out to be some women from a nearby camp defecating behind a thorn bush.

I knew it was madness but I couldn't stop and the others were equally possessed, avid to find and run down. Kulutan avid to prove himself right and damn Amodi once and for all.

Was he lying, Kulutan?

I was trembling with sheer fear and a mad cold jealous need to find out the truth. How would I dare to confront it if we did find them? At the back of my mind was some awareness of the obscene flagrant injustice of what we were doing, like the hunters who chased gazelles in Landrovers, running them over in their bloodlust.

Then the car began to jolt and I thought that we had run something over and for a sickening mad moment of horror imagined Amodi's body beneath our wheels, blood seeping through white cloth.

When Haruna stopped and groaned and turned the engine off I didn't interpret it easily as I normally would.

We all sat staring at him questioningly.

"It's the fucking tyre," he said. "And I've left the jack back at the camp. I had it out and I forgot to put it back in the car when all those fucking Buzus came and that elephant of a woman."

I wasn't surprised to see three figures returning where two had set out – Sideka surely, I thought, as I stared through the dusty darkness.

"Welcome!" Ilyas shouted. But they didn't respond.

It was Sideka. When they drew near the solemnity of their faces startled me.

Haruna came up and dropped the jack and a *bidon* of water on the sand with a thud. But he said nothing, just stood there hands on hips, feet firmly planted, eyes downcast.

Kulutan dropped to a squat beside me. His breathing was a bit ragged. "There is bad news," he said.

I waited.

"There has been trouble in Tchin Tabaraden."

Sideka joined him. "It is said some young men attacked the police post and some police were killed. Earlier tonight."

The starkness of that. The stark simplicity of that.

"What young men?"

"Some who had been to Libya – and others."

"It is said Libya helped them. Gave them the guns," said Sideka.

"Ellen," said Haruna, "they are saying back at the camp that Amodi was there. Maybe."

*No. Ridiculous.*

"No one knows where he is," said Sideka.

"They're mad," said Kulutan. "What does Amodi know of Libya or guns? I tell you Amodi is somewhere here in this desert!"

I felt like a trapped bird. "What of the young men? Were any of them killed?" *The bloody stupid bastard young fools.*

"Yes, indeed, some were."

"The people are scared, Ellen," said Haruna. "They've stopped drumming. They're all packing off home." He heaved the tool-box from the car. "Even the elephant woman."

"They're afraid, if any of the young men who were in it have escaped, the police will come looking for them," said Kulutan.

"I must get back and check for Amodi." I could hear the trace of hysteria in my voice.

"Right, let's work," said Haruna, straining to loosen a nut. "Hey, Buzu, until you help me with these nuts."

Kulutan pulled off his *tagilmoust* and laid it aside, then pulled his white robe off over his head. He wore a belt with a long knife in a decorated scabbard. Taking off the belt and knife he laid them on the bundled-up robe. He joined Haruna and muscles rippled as he spun the wrench, loosening a nut like making butter curls.

Jacking the car up on the soft yielding sand was difficult as always. Twice it collapsed and eventually, as they removed the wheel with the jack precariously poised, it shifted and my heart jolted with it as it shuddered but then held. I held my breath as Haruna twirled off the nuts they had already loosened and removed the wheel.

He and Kulutan attacked the tyre with the tyre irons.

*"What are you doing?"* I shrieked. *"You're not going to mend that now! Put the bloody spare wheel on until we get back to camp!"*

Haruna straightened up and looked at me, shamefaced. "It has a puncture, Ellen. We had a slow puncture earlier and I changed the wheel. That's why I had the jack out back at camp."

"You put it on the back without mending it."

He nodded.

As I stared at him, speechless in frustration, there was an interruption from Ilyas.

*"God forbid!"* Ilyas had frozen. He was gazing into the darkness back in the direction of the camp.

"Kulutan, look!" said Sideka sharply.

There in the far distance but distinct enough for me to see, was a moving reflection against the sky. Like a miniature *Son et Lumiére*.

"What is it?" I asked as Kulutan dropped his tyre iron and stared like the others.

"Cars," said Sideka in a voice without expression but his face was full of fear.

"For God's sake!" said Haruna. "Help me with this fucking tyre!"

But the other three were like deer scenting the hunter, frozen, poised for flight.

"Boys," said Kulutan quietly, "you proceed with the work. Until I go back to see what has happened." He rose and, taking his knife and belt, he strode off. I watched as his dark skin and black trousers melted into the darkness.

He had only just disappeared when the first gunshots sounded.

The boys were working feverishly on the damaged inner tube. They had found a massive thorn in it and repaired the hole. When they pumped it, it held. But then Haruna turned from preparing the tyre to find the tube had perceptibly deflated.

"In the name of God, a slow puncture," said Haruna. And began a search for the second hole with the aid of the water from the *bidon* poured into a calabash, watching for bubbles by torchlight.

There had been other shots and now, when another distant burst of gunfire cracked in the distance, Sideka leapt to his feet and, his voice full of tears, said, "I'm going!"

"Sideka! Sideka!" I called after him and began to run, hampered by the little gazelle in my arms. "Don't go! Kulutan will be back now! Sideka!"

He looked over his shoulder and began to trot as he saw me catching up on him, soon leaving me behind.

I was some distance from the car. My chest heaved. I walked another bit forward, straining my eyes, praying to see not just Sideka but Kulutan returning. I had no idea whatsoever how long it had taken the boys to walk to the camp and return the last time. It could have been fifteen minutes, or thirty or an hour.

I began to walk a little faster and farther, clutching Zincad, looking back all the time to keep myself in line with the car. I could no longer really see it in the dusty distance.

There was a little bunch of thorn and acacia trees ahead of me, looming out of the gloom. I stopped. And waited. I prayed, muttering frantically *Hail Mary, Full of Grace, The Lord is with Thee, Blessed art Thou amongst women . . .* I couldn't remember the rest – what came next? *Blessed art Thou amongst women and . . .* and what? If I couldn't remember, the worst would happen.

What was that? There was a splay of light wavering to my left, the faint hum of a vehicle. My heart was in my throat. Then the light disappeared. I gabbled it over and over again but came to a halt each time.

I couldn't remember. I shifted prayers: *Hail Holy Queen, Mother of Mercy, Hail our Life, our Sweetness and Our Hope. To Thee do we cry, poor banished Children of Eve, To Thee do we send up our sighs, mourning and weeping in this valley of tears . . . Turn then . . .*

How long had I waited already? If I waited for them, how long would it be? Could they have circled back and gone back to the Land Cruiser?

I couldn't bear it.

I moved forward another few hundred yards. Lights still flared against the sky but stronger now that I was a little bit nearer. And now I could hear women wailing.

I stood and strained my eyes and prayed for a long time.

I put Zincad down and she began to cry, so I picked her up again.

I moved forward, sheltering in the thick thorn brush, and kept moving steadily until I could see the eyes of the circle of Landrovers like monstrous animals crouching in the dark and within their scope, a floodlit arena.

And soldiers stood here and there, guns poised, bodies thick and heavy in combat gear.

The black-robed figure of a woman crouched to one side wailing over a figure on the ground. Who?

In the centre of the arena were three soldiers, before them a naked grey-bearded man. I thought it was Abu Bakr but I couldn't be sure.

I wanted to move, to rush forward, but I could not shake off the sheer terror that made my blood turn to ice. In my head, I went in there screaming, blind in red-hot rage. But I couldn't move for the crushing paralysis of fear.

Rage came easily to me. One day in Tanout, I'd seen a soldier force a young Tuareg girl to her feet – she had been crouched on the ground, struck with labour pains and about to miscarry when he had decided the sight was offensive. As two women hauled, almost dragged her away, I scooped up a handful of sand and threw it in his face in my rage. His fellow-soldiers had restrained him from laying me out with the butt of his machine-gun.

But this was atavistic terror not atavistic rage. It kept me frozen in place. Next it would catapult me into flight.

I fought against it as I had fought the spirits earlier that night, my limbs leaden and rooted again.

And again, like a nightmare repeating, an arm was about my waist and a hand was on me, over my mouth, and

Kulutan's face again was close like a face in dream. He half-carried me away, my lips beneath his hand crushed against my teeth, blood salty in my mouth.

After a while, he set me down and tried to take the gazelle from my arms but I held it so forcefully he could not and I was unable to open my arms.

I wanted to ask about Amodi, about Sideka, but a passion of flight overrode love and care. We fled, he supporting me, keeping my balance for me as I stumbled on legs that shook so much I thought my joints were about to slide out of place.

By the time we came upon the Land Cruiser I could feel the blood racing through my body again, could hear my painful ragged breath, could feel anger redden my mind.

I thought Yassine was cradling a butchered and skinned kid when I saw her sitting on the sand, supported by Sideka'a encircling arm. I fell on my knees before her, at last letting the gazelle go. I put my hand on her wrapper where it pooled blackly on the ground. And my hand sunk moistly into the sand. I raised it and it was bright with blood in the dim moonlight. Dully, I stared and saw the black pool was blood. The little carcass in her arms was clothed in blood from a deep gouge in the throat but Raechitu's little face was unbloodied, tranquil in death. Yassine was silent. I embraced her, my head against hers, and my tears ran down her cold forehead. I didn't know until she slumped backwards against our arms with a groan that the blood pooling on the sand was coming from her.

We lay her down, Raechitu slipping from her arms to lie across the pulsing gash in her mother's belly.

Yassine's face was a pale bloodless oval.

"She is dead," said Sideka.

Yes, though I could still see the pulse in her neck.

Her pale lips moved the faintest bit and then were still. Her hands trailed slackly from her baby's body.

"They found us . . . in the bush," said Sideka, his breath harsh in his throat. "I met her outside the camp . . . she had gone to urinate . . . "

"Yes? Yes?" I said sharply in English. *Tell me quickly.*

"I was bringing her back here . . . when one Landrover came from the east. I took Muhane and ran . . . " He gestured behind him and I saw Muhane sitting on the sand by the Land Cruiser, huddled in a little ball, arms over her head. "They caught Yassine . . . when I went back they had already left. She was naked. They had forced her and . . . " His lips worked dryly trying to speak again but he could not.

Behind him, Haruna and Kulutan were working furiously, taking it in turns to pump the wheel.

"Enough, Kulutan, enough!" Haruna took the wheel and bounced it off the ground. Kulutan leant his weight on it. It held.

With infinite care they placed it on the hub, hardly breathing, afraid to unbalance the jack, and then began to twirl the nuts back into place.

"We must run away, Ellen," said Kulutan, gasping. "Do you understand that they will kill you if they find you here? They won't want a foreign witness."

He was right.

And I realised that, mercifully, we had come through In-Gall and the Tchin Tabaraden police did not know we were here.

Unless someone had told them.

*Like Amodi?*

No. No. Amodi was with Lella somewhere in this desert.

"Come! Come!" Kulutan grabbed me roughly by the arm. Ilyas was already swinging the little tangle of limbs that was Muhane into the back of the car.

"Yassine," I said. "We must take Yassine."

"She's dead, Ellen," said Kulutan gently.

Haruna was in the driving-seat. "Hurry!"

"Don't turn on the lights, Haruna!" Kulutan pushed me up into the passenger seat and climbed in beside me. "Haruna! If we push the car a little distance there is a place over there where the land falls away a little. It is better to do that lest they hear the engine."

"Ellen!" said Haruna, jumping out of the car.

Which would waste more time? My weight in the car as they tried to push or the care they would have to take if I helped to push and Haruna were trying to steer it from outside?

I scrambled into the driving-seat and released the brake.

We were moving. Slowly, heavily, bogged in sand. Only desperation could have moved it on such a surface. Then perhaps the sand grew more compact and we were moving more easily. I glanced back at Muhane and was confronted by a stark little face, smeared with tears and blood and mucous, close to mine.

Suddenly the ground gave way quite steeply.

"Get in! Get in!" I shouted but then realised in the same moment that they couldn't do that without ruining our momentum. The Land Cruiser ran rapidly down the incline. The ground levelled out a bit but we continued to move for quite a long time. When we at last crept to a halt there was neither sight nor sound of the others and it was a little while before I saw them running in our wake.

The first sound of the engine when Haruna turned the key seemed to shatter the night but as we moved on it was almost drowned out by the throbbing of my heart and the blood in my ears.

The car was a beloved throbbing living creature carrying us to safety. Leaving Amodi. Leaving Ataka.

We drove on silently, faces gleaming with sweat, and Tazerza was far behind when, with a sickening jolt of the stomach, I remembered the gazelle.

"Zincad, we forgot her, the *zincad*." And a wash of pain and guilt flooded through me as if it were the ultimate betrayal.

"She's here, Ellen," said Sideka, voice thick with tears. "I brought her for you."

And he handed the little gazelle over the seatback to me.

I took it with relief and cradled it against my belly, a curving delicate little exile, twin of the child who lay curled inside me, waiting to be born into a harsh world.

# Prologue/Epilogue

*Croagh Patrick, Mayo, West of Ireland*

The mist swirled around the summit, clearing for brief snatches of breathtaking sunlit views.

My feet still felt okay, surprisingly, and I felt elated.

People milled about, some purposefully – still counting circuits and *Our Father's* and *Hail Mary's* no doubt – others as aimlessly as myself.

Mass was being said in a little stone chapel. The donkeys

that had borne the priest and his sacred hosts to the summit before daybreak (had they carried up the Coca-Cola at the same time?) were patiently standing nearby.

I watched a headscarved old woman reach out in reverent triumph to touch the large cross that marked the highest point, her rosary beads swinging from the reaching hand. The mist swirled. A camera clicked. A professional. He smiled smugly, job done. He had taken it against the light. Black and white, in dramatic silhouette the old woman would adorn the front page of some national newspaper the following day – an image to reprimand and reassure a smug pagan nation over breakfast:

*I should have been there – but, aren't we great all the same? The Irish never lost it – where else would you find the likes of that? 'Tis great the old traditions are being kept up – I must do it meself – one of these years . . .*

I emerged from the mist and went a few yards further down the side of the mountain. I took off my back-pack and sat down gratefully.

I had another ritual to fulfil. I fumbled in my back-pack and pulled out a bunch of envelopes. Petitions. Sealed. There was my sister's. I stared at it, avid and yet reluctant to know what was inside. I wanted to look but I was scared. What if it said: *God give me patience to put up with my sister Ellen . . .*

I stuck it into the little pile out of temptation's way.

The mottled grey – that was my mother's. I knew what that would say: all my mother's prayers and petitions were the same – it would be a prayer for the protection and happiness of her daughters.

I picked out one small violet envelope, a stylishly

decorated *Petition* written on it in a teenage hand. This was my daughter's. Her name is Yassine.

This, I would look at – for better or worse. How to help fulfil her dreams – dreams that flowed powerfully in great subterranean depths beneath her African calm – if I didn't know what they were?

I held the envelope with hands that were suddenly sticky with sweat. My breath came short and my eyes seemed to blur with tension as I stared at the envelope as though I could read through it.

But why open it? I knew what this one would say too.

The little gazelle had died, choking on the mucous of the humidity of Nigeria. I had let it die. I still felt the guilt of it.

But the child inside me had lived. Somehow that seemed not right, so much had I identified the little animal with the new life in me.

Out of its natural element of drought and desert, the gazelle had died. But my child had thrived. As had Yassine's little Muhane.

While the storm settled over Niger, while the ancient boils were lanced, while all I knew there was shattered. But I mustn't think of that. I must never think of that.

It would have been good if the gazelle had lived.

The significance of things can only evolve in time. Nothing is what it is until it becomes what it must become. I thought of Lawrence . . . *TE, what happened "curled up in a knot" under those goatskin cloaks under the top of Mount Hor? Whatever happened became in time the whole of the Arab revolt and ended in the blood and pain of floggings in darkest Dorset. I offered a green apple to a tinker girl on an icy morning in Cork, with your book under my arm; and Yassine died.*

I took the little envelope and, scrabbling about among the stones, thrust it deep with the other envelopes into a little rocky tomb.

Maybe I should have taken it to some other shrine in Ireland, one of the ones where prayers were speared on the branches of trees, so that my daughter's prayer could speak more clearly across space to that other charm suspended in the thorn tree in the Sahara. If it was still there.

I bowed my head, summoned up my spirit and said my own prayer.

Then I shoved myself to my feet with the help of the pilgrim staff and started to make my way, on now trembling and exhausted muscles, kneecaps almost threatening to give way and slide out of place, back down the mountain.

I couldn't see any of the people who had been with me on the bus.

I felt a little stab of panic – I was very late. My bare feet had slowed me down. I hoped the bus would wait.

⚜⚜⚜

*Le Figaro 16/6/90*

# NIGER
## MASSACRES OF TUAREGS IN NIGER

*Some hundreds of Nigerien Tuaregs have been*
*massacred, by the Nigerien army, in the region*
*of Tchin Tabaraden: the information, first*
*published by* Le Monde, *has been confirmed by*
Le Figaro *through an authorised source in Niger.*
*There have also been recorded numerous cases of*
*rape and torture . . .*
*The Head of State has invited Amnesty*
*International to come and "make their count".*

Published by Poolbeg

# POLYGAMY

*by*

## GAYE SHORTLAND

"*I watched Khadija. I wanted to be comforted like the children. I wanted to grasp her golden breasts with their dusky overlay of indigo. I wanted to lay my head on her rounded thighs and breathe in that musky mix of indigo and sweat and oil-based perfume – his smell – the smell of his tribe.*"

Set in Nigeria and French Niger on the edge of the Sahara, *Polygamy* is a vivid story of love, betrayal and joy by the highly acclaimed author of *Mind That 'tis My Brother* and *Turtles All the Way Down*.

"Shortland leaves the reader dumbstruck, so striking are her images, so vivid her characters."

Siobhan Long, *Hot Press*

"The clash of cultures on the sexual plain I have not seen drawn so starkly before."

Michael Carson, Author of *Sucking Sherbet Lemons* and *Dying in Style*

ISBN 1-85371-852-1

Published by Poolbeg

# TURTLES ALL THE WAY DOWN

*by*

## GAYE SHORTLAND

*"Yeh could say the honeymoon was ovur. To tell yeh the truth I was pissed off. Isn't human nature a queer thing? You'll grant me 'human nature', I hope? Dead an all as I am?"*

Tony, "the only survivor of AIDS unknown to modern medicine", last encountered as ashes in an urn in *Mind That 'tis My Brother*, emerges here as a free spirit with "no visible means of support" and a serious case of angst.

His attempt to discover the meaning of death in Cork City (while performing as Guardian Angel to his beloved Declan and friends of assorted genders) is sabotaged by TVs, turtles, and the Guinness Jazz Trail, and a tendency to slip off to the jungles of Indo-China where he is side-kick to Major O'Hara, a man's man and "the very head off Clint Eastwood".

But Tony is a survivor. He hangs in there to the bitter end . . .

ISBN 1-85371-699-5